MARINELLI Carol
More Precious Than A Crown

CLASS NO.

TO AVOID OVERDUE CHARGES THIS BOOK SHOULD BE
RETURNED ON OR BEFORE THE LAST DATE STAMPED
ABOVE. IF NOT REQUIRED BY ANOTHER READER IT MAY
BE RENEWED BY PERSONAL CALL, TELEPHONE OR POST.

MORE PRECIOUS
THAN A CROWN

MORE PRECIOUS THAN A CROWN

BY
CAROL MARINELLI

First published in Great Britain 2014
by Mills & Boon, an imprint of Harlequin (UK) Limited,
Large Print edition 2015
Eton House, 18-24 Paradise Road,
Richmond, Surrey, TW9 1SR

© 2014 Carol Marinelli

ISBN: 978-0-263-25583-6

Printed and bound in Great Britain
by CPI Antony Rowe, Chippenham, Wiltshire

To my lovely Facebook friends,
who cheer me on when my heroes misbehave.

PROLOGUE

'HAS ANYONE SEEN TRINITY?'

Dianne's voice carried through the still night.
It had become a familiar cry this past year or
so, and one that Sheikh Prince Zahid of Ishla
had grown more than a little used to whenever
he spent time at the Fosters' residence.

Zahid had been a regular guest to the house-
hold since he had been sixteen but now, about
to turn twenty-two, he had made the decision
that this would be his last time he would stay
here. The next time he was invited he would
politely decline.

Zahid walked through the woods at the edge
of the Foster property. He could hear the sounds
of laughter carry across the lake on this clear
summer night. Zahid was flying back to Ishla
soon and he hoped that his driver would arrive
early rather than promptly, for he really would

rather not be here. The Fosters were throwing a party to celebrate their son Donald's graduation and, given that they had added the fact that Zahid too was graduating, it would have been rude to decline.

Next time he would.

Zahid did not enjoy their company, he never really had. Gus Foster was a politician and it seemed to Zahid that he never switched off. His wife Dianne's sole purpose in life seemed to be to stand by her man whatever Gus did. Since Zahid had known the family, there had been the humiliation of two very public affairs as well as the scandalous revelations of sleazier encounters and not once had Dianne's plastic smile wavered.

After tonight he would not have to see it again, Zahid thought. Neither would he have to make polite small talk with the obnoxious Gus. He only did it because he was a friend of their son Donald.

Well, as much as Zahid had friends.

Zahid was a lone wolf and very independent. He preferred the company of a beautiful woman on a Saturday night rather than this type of thing, but obligation had brought him here.

When he had been sixteen and a boarder at a top school there had been a random locker inspection and a wad of cash and drugs had been found in Zahid's locker. They had not been Zahid's. It hadn't been the mandatory suspension that had been the problem, though. It had been the deep shame that such a scandal would cause his family.

On hearing the news, Zahid's father, King Fahid, had immediately boarded his jet to fly from Ishla to speak with the headmaster, not to cover things up, for that was not how things worked in Ishla. Instead, Zahid had explained to Donald, the king was on his way to England to apologise and take his disgraced son home. Once in Ishla, Zahid would have to publicly apologise to the people of Ishla.

'Even if you didn't do it?' Donald had asked.

Zahid had nodded.

'It is up to the people if they forgive me.'

Zahid had stepped into the headmaster's office with his back straight and his head held high, ready to meet his fate, only to find out that there had been a misunderstanding.

Donald, the headmaster had informed the prince and king, on hearing about the locker inspection, had panicked and placed the money and drugs in Zahid's. It was Donald who would now be suspended and the school offered its sincere apologies for the disruption the incident had caused the king.

As the king and young prince had stepped out of the headmaster's office, there had stood Donald with his father, Gus.

'Thank you,' King Fahid had said to Donald, 'for being man enough to admit the error of your ways.'

'You miss the point,' Gus had said to the king. 'My son would never do drugs, he did this to help a friend.'

The Fosters had taken it on the chin.

Gus had even given a speech in Parliament, stating that even the most loving, functional families were not exempt from the perils of teenage years.

Functional?

Zahid had frowned at the choice of word then and was frowning now as he walked, recalling that time all those years ago.

The Fosters had appeared on the front pages on the Sunday newspapers. Dianne, smiling her plastic smile for the cameras, Gus with his arm around his suitably sheepish-looking son. The only one who had spoiled the picture-perfect image had been Trinity—she had been dressed in her Sunday best but, rather than smiling, she had scowled at the cameras.

Zahid actually smiled as he recalled the photo from yesteryear but he wasn't smiling a few seconds later when a streak of blonde caught his eye.

There was Trinity.

She was hiding a bag of clothes beneath a tree and wiping lipstick off, and jumped when she heard Zahid call out and start walking towards her.

'Trinity!' Zahid said. 'Your mother has been calling for you. Where have you been?'

She swung around to face him. 'Please, Zahid, can I say that I've been with you?'

'You know I don't lie.'

'Please,' Trinity said, and then sighed. Zahid was so austere, so formal and so rigid that it was pointless even trying to get him on side. Yet, just as she went to walk off and face the music, he halted her.

'If I am going to cover for you, first I need to know what you have been up to.'

Trinity slowly turned. Even when she had asked Zahid to cover for her, she'd never really expected him to agree, yet it sounded now like he might. 'I was at my friend Suzanne's,' came her cautious reply.

'Doing what?'

'Just…' Trinity shrugged.

'Just what?'

'Dancing.'

'You have been to a party?'

'No! We were just listening to music in her

room and dancing.' Trinity almost rolled her eyes as she attempted to explain to his non-plussed expression, because clearly that wasn't the type of behaviour Zahid would understand. 'We were trying on make-up, that sort of thing.'

'Why are you hiding clothes?' Zahid looked at what she was wearing—a long-sleeved top and a pair of jeans—and then he watched as Trinity screwed her blue eyes closed, no doubt to come up with a suitable lie.

Trinity was, Zahid knew, a skilled liar, only what he didn't know was that she wasn't try-ing to lie now. She simply didn't know, in this, how she could tell the truth, when it was just a feeling she had.

How could she explain that Suzanne had suggested she borrow some clothes because Trinity hadn't liked the way her aunt's new husband had been looking at her in the dress her mother had bought for her? Trinity didn't understand enough herself, let alone know how to explain it to Zahid, just how awkward Clive made her feel.

She refused to call him Uncle.

He was the reason that she'd run off.

It was the reason that Trinity was always running off at family things and, given that Zahid was only ever there on family occasions, he saw this behaviour all too often.

'Last time I was here, I caught you climbing out of your bedroom window,' Zahid said, and watched as Trinity did her very best to keep her face straight. 'It is not a laughing matter.'

No, it wasn't a laughing matter, Trinity thought, but the memory of it made her smile. Zahid had refused to believe she had simply been hungry and, rather than facing all the guests, had simply been trying to sneak into the kitchen. He'd brought her out a plate of food and then watched as she'd climbed back up to her room, using a tree and the trellis. Given her practised movements, it had been a presumably well-worn path for Trinity.

'I haven't done anything wrong,' Trinity said.

'Perhaps not, but on family occasions you should be here.' It was black and white to Zahid yet sometimes with Trinity it blurred to grey. She was so spirited and wilful and just so visibly unimpressed with her family that at times she made Zahid silently cheer, not that he would let her know that. 'You don't just disappear.'

'I know, I know,' Trinity started, but then a mischievous smile prettied her sulky face. 'So, what's your excuse, then?'

'Excuse?'

'What are you doing in the woods?' And then, as realisation hit, she started to laugh. 'Sorry, that was a stupid question.' Zahid's frown only deepened the more she tried to explain. 'Well, I guess you needed to...' Trinity stopped then. There was not a single vulgar thing about Zahid and, no, now that she came to think of it, Trinity could not imagine Zahid popping into the woods to answer the call of nature! 'My mistake.'

'I went for a walk so that I could think.' Zahid looked down at her. Of all the Fosters, Trinity was the only one he would miss. Yes, she made him smile at times, but he wasn't smiling as he saw that since her last escapade Trinity had changed. She had, in fact, grown into a very beautiful young woman. Her hair was blonde and had been cut in a jagged style, her eyes were huge in a too-thin face and they sparkled as she waited for him to speak. 'If you were in Ishla you would be expected to support your parents and mix with the guests...'

'I'm not in Ishla, though.'

As they started to walk back towards the party, Trinity tripped a little.

'Have you been drinking?'

'No.'

'Are you sure?'

'I think I'd remember if I had.'

He turned her to him and took her cheeks in his hands. He saw her dilated pupils and neither quite recognised the lust between them yet. 'Blow.'

'You're breath-testing me?'

'Blow,' Zahid said, and she did, but he could smell no alcohol.

'What are you up to, Trinity?' Zahid asked,

except his hands did not leave her face and neither did Trinity want them to. Yes, he was boring, yes, he was yawn-yawn dignified, but sometimes when he smiled, sometimes when his subtle humour went completely over her parents' heads, he made her laugh. She had never understood what women saw in him. Donald was bitterly jealous and complained often to his family that women only went after Zahid for his title.

Tonight Trinity would beg to differ.

Now she understood his attraction, for those black eyes made the skin on her cheeks flare with heat and the height of him, instead of intimidating her, had her wanting to stand on tiptoe and lift her face to his like a flower to the sun.

Now they recognised the lust.

Zahid looked down at her. She was like a little wild kitten that any minute might scratch but right now was temporarily tame, and Zahid was knocked sideways by her appeal.

'Am I to breathe out again...?' Trinity said,

and as he went to open his mouth to tell her they should get back, Trinity blew into his open mouth. He captured her breath and then swallowed, and for the first time Zahid wrestled with self-control.

'You need to be more careful,' Zahid warned. 'You should not be walking alone in the woods at night.'

'In case a handsome prince happens to be walking by?'

'I could be anyone,' Zahid pointed out, but his hands were still on her cheeks.

Their lips were almost touching.

'You're you,' Trinity said, 'and I want you to give me my first kiss.'

Her mouth was, to Zahid, perfect and he was, rarely for him, tentative as his lips grazed hers for he was wrestling for control, forcing himself to hold back not just want, for the pulse of her flesh on his lips gave him more than the usual want, it filled him with need, and a man of Zahid's standing must never feel need that wasn't met.

For Trinity to feel him kiss her so tenderly, to feel that sulky mouth now soft against hers, was sublime.

A late developer, for six months now, or perhaps a little more, Trinity had loathed her body. The feel of another's eyes on her had made her feel ill. Family functions had been spent fighting hands that wandered, yet she was not fighting hands now. She loved the feel of Zahid's hands moving from her cheeks and down to her waist, and when her lips parted the slip of tongues was so mutual, so natural that Trinity let out a moan.

Zahid would have loved to linger, she tasted of cinnamon and was so sweet and warm, but the purr of her too-thin body beneath his hands, the sudden tip into sexual hunger from Trinity, the raw need in himself were enough for Zahid to attempt to halt things.

'That was not your first kiss.' His voice was not accusing, he was merely stating a fact, for never had a mouth had such an effect on him before and surely it had been a practised kiss.

'Okay, it was my second,' Trinity admitted. 'Suzanne and I practised a while back so that we'd know what we were doing, but this doesn't feel like practice, though,' she breathed, her mouth searching for his again.

'You need to get back,' Zahid said. His voice was just a touch stern, for he was cross at his own lack of control. His life was ordered, the women he dated were generally a few years older than him, not the other way around, and with reason, for emotion he kept at a distance and love was something to actively avoid.

Sex was the name of the game but it felt like more than that now.

Trinity's hands met at the back of his neck and she looked up at him. His hands were just above her hips and she knew that at any moment they would disengage, that he would take her back, but Trinity didn't want that. She wanted her first proper kiss to go on for longer, she did not want to return to her family and the house, but more than that, she wanted more time with Zahid.

He was far too tall for her mouth to reach his without Zahid lowering his head, so when still he did not, her mouth moved to his neck, and worked upwards, inhaling his lovely scent and feeling his hands digging deeper into her hips.

There was a strange push-pull, for he should push her off, take her hand and walk back, yet Zahid was resisting the urge to pull her into his groin. Trinity's tongue licked up his neck and then one hand did move. Zahid took her chin in his fingers and Trinity blinked up at him. She thought for a moment that she was about to be told off, but instead his mouth came down on hers and she found out that the first kiss had been but a precursor to bliss.

Trinity's eyes snapped open at the passion behind his kiss. She was a little shocked, a little heady and then, when she saw the usually remote Zahid so consumed, Trinity's eyes closed again and just revelled in the bliss of being so thoroughly kissed. One of his hands was stroking her hip and his tongue was sliding around hers and there was nothing but pleasure to be had. His other hand was on her shoulder but almost pushing her back in an attempt to resist pulling her in, yet it was Trinity who ignored the pressure and moved a delicious bit closer and discovered her home.

In the circle of his arms, pressed against him, she found herself.

Trinity loved the feel of his sex against her stomach and finally the bliss of the pressure of his hand pulling her in as his tongue duelled with hers. Now she moved up on tiptoe, wanting to feel that delicious hard length lower yet. Still fighting himself, Zahid pushed her down. It was like a match to gasoline for Trinity and she rose to her toes again and then it was she who pushed down and Zahid wrenched his face back, ending the kiss but not the contact of their groins, his dark eyes assessing her but with a smile on that stern mouth, which was shiny from hers.

'Don't stop,' Trinity urged, pressing herself to him, She was building towards something that felt like a faint wail of sirens in the vague distance. Her body was on delicious alert, seeking their direction, as Zahid did his best to contain her.

'We shall stop,' Zahid said.

'Why?'

'Because…' Zahid did not want to stop, but neither did he want to continue things here. 'Because my driver shall be here soon to take me back to Ishla, and you are too good for the woods.'

'Take me back to your palace.' Trinity smiled but then it disappeared, a note of urgency creeping into her voice. 'I need to get away…'

Zahid frowned. 'When you say—' He never got to finish, Dianne's shrill voice terminating their conversation.

'There you are. What the hell…?'

Zahid dropped contact as soon as he realised that her mother was there but Trinity still hung like a cheeky monkey around his neck.

'Mrs Foster, I apologise. I was—'

'Oh, it's you! It's fine, Zahid.' Dianne was instantly mollified when she saw that it was

Zahid who her daughter was with. 'Zahid, your driver is here and, Trinity, you need to come and say goodbye to our guests...' They walked back through the woods and towards the house, Zahid frowning at Dianne's rather inappropriate response—surely she should be furious but she was chatting away as if nothing had happened. 'Clive and Elaine are staying. Trinity, I want you to go and get the guest room ready.'

His driver was waiting and he pulled Zahid aside to tell him that if he wanted to fly tonight, they needed to leave now.

Zahid said swift goodbyes, but Trinity caught his hand and he could see the tears filling her eyes.

'Zahid, what I said about you taking me with you. Do you think maybe—?'

'Trinity.' He could have kicked himself. She was reading far too much into one kiss and he had never meant to confuse her. He was just glad that Dianne had disturbed them when she had.

'I have to go.' Zahid's words were a touch

abrupt but better that than she even glimpse the effect she had had on him.

Her hand gripped his fingers and he felt the brush of her fingertips as he pulled away from her and glanced at his watch.

It was ten minutes after eleven and as he climbed into his car, little did he know that it was a moment in time he would regret for ever.

He looked out of the window and cursed his brief lack of control as the car pulled off.

It was better that he return now to Ishla, Zahid decided, for he did not like her unsettling effect on him.

Yet it was one kiss that he would always remember.

As for Trinity...

She saw his car drive off and on her mother's orders headed back into the house to prepare the guest room.

Trinity too would never forget that night.

But for all the wrong reasons.

CHAPTER ONE

'DECLINE.'

Sheikh Prince Zahid's response was immediate.

The king, his son and Abdul, the king's chief aide, were walking through the second palace of Ishla, discussing the refurbishments that were necessary if it were to be inhabited again. As they walked Abdul discussed the diaries of the royal prince and king and raised the matter of Donald Foster's wedding.

The Fosters had always imbued a certain discomfort in Zahid—loud, brash, their egos and need to further themselves at all costs had not sat comfortably with Zahid. As he had matured he had done his best to politely sever contact but Donald had remained persistent and they still occasionally kept in touch.

'But Donald has asked you to be his best man.'

Zahid's jaw tightened a fraction as Abdul spoke on. Zahid had not told his father that just last week Donald had called, asking him if he would be his best man at his wedding to Yvette. Zahid had said to Donald that, while flattered, he had duties in his homeland at that time and would not be able to attend. He had rather hoped that that would be the end of it, but of course Donald had persisted and it would now appear that a formal invitation had been sent, along with a repeated request that Zahid be Donald's best man. 'I have already explained that I cannot attend his wedding,' Zahid said to Abdul. 'Offer my apologies and arrange a gift...'

'Donald Foster?' The King halted and turned round and Zahid silently cursed Abdul for insisting that they go through the diaries now. He had been hoping that his father would not find out. 'That is the man who saved our family from shame...'

'That was a very long time ago, Father.'

'Our country has a long memory,' the king responded. 'You owe that man...'

'I have more than repaid my debt to him.'

Over and over Zahid had repaid his debt to Donald—he had been his friend when, perhaps, Zahid would rather not have been, he had secured invitations to functions that Donald would never have got into had he not asked Zahid to intervene, and over the years Donald had also borrowed significant amounts of money and made no effort to pay him back.

'Were it not for Donald,' the king pointed out, 'you would have been brought into disrepute. More than that, you would have brought our country into disrepute. When is the wedding?'

'It is in two weeks,' Abdul said, then looked at Zahid. 'We could rearrange your schedule.'

'First a wedding and, given the speed it's been arranged, soon it will be a christening...' Zahid pointed out, and the King tutted.

'I would support a polite declining of your attendance at a christening for a child conceived out of wedlock, as would our people, but the wedding...'

To the king's surprise, Zahid took no more

persuading, for he interrupted with a brief nod and then turned to Abdul. 'Very well, arrange my schedule but make it a brief visit, two nights at the most. I will fly out the day after the wedding.'

'If only it were that easy to get you to agree to more pressing matters,' Fahid commented, but Zahid did not respond, for he knew what was coming next—his father had brought him here for a reason, Zahid was sure. 'We need to speak about the renovations that are needed here.'

Memories stirred for both the king and Abdul as they walked through the second jewel of Ishla. The second palace was where Zahid and his sister Layla had been born and raised. Even on their mother's death, when Zahid had been seven, they had lived here. The king had been heartbroken at the death of his wife, Annan, but thanks to the privacy the second palace had afforded them, he had been able to grieve largely in private.

Zahid deliberately kept his face impassive as they discussed the work that needed doing, but he knew that just the fact his father had chosen to speak with him here meant that the reins were tightening.

His father had long since wanted him to choose a suitable bride. So far Zahid had resisted, he liked his freedom far too much, but this was a working royal family and Zahid's skills in engineering were being utilised, his vision for Ishla was taking shape, and more and more his time was spent here.

It was time for Zahid to raise a family.

'There is much work to be done,' Abdul said. 'The chief architect is concerned about some erosion on the cliff face and, as we thought, the great hall and the master suite are in need of structural repair.'

'How long will that take?'

'Six months to a year is his best estimate,' Abdul said, and went into further detail. It wasn't as simple as commencing work—the second palace contained many valuable pieces that would need to be catalogued and stored before work could even begin.

'You do realise, Zahid,' the king said to his eldest son, 'that once it gets out that activity has commenced at the second place, our people will assume that we are preparing the palace for the crown prince and his bride.'

'I do,' Zahid replied.

'And does six months to one year sound like a time-frame you could operate within?'

Black eyes met black eyes and there was a small stand-off. The king had raised a leader, which meant Zahid would not simply be told what he should do.

'I think that at this stage, it would be premature to go ahead with the renovations.' Zahid did not flinch as he defied his father's request that he marry soon.

'Your country wants to know that they have a prince who will—'

'They have a prince,' Zahid calmly interrupted, 'who shall one day rule fairly and wisely. I do not need a bride to assure them of that.'

'You need an heir,' the king said. 'If something should happen to you, they need to know that the line will continue.' He let out an irritated breath. Zahid refused to be pushed into anything, which the king grudgingly admired, but the people needed reassuring. Time was running out for the king and so he chose now to play the one card he had that just might persuade Zahid to submit to his will. 'Of course, should something happen to you, it would be Layla's son who would be next in line.'

Zahid's jaw gritted because Layla did not have a husband, let alone a son.

'Perhaps,' the king continued, 'if the crown prince chooses not to marry yet, another royal wedding might appease the people.'

'Father...' Zahid addressed him as a father and not a king, trying to reach for his softer side, for the king truly adored his daughter. 'Layla does not like any of her prospective husbands.'

'Layla needs to understand that with privilege comes responsibility. I am thinking of inviting the Fayeds to dine here at the palace next week.'

Zahid thought about Layla, who had kicked,

screamed and bitten when her father had once attempted to drag her out to meet suitors.

She was a rebel, a challenge, and reminded him of...

Perhaps it was the wedding invitation but Zahid's mind drifted back in time and he recalled Trinity. Not the kiss but the fire in her eyes and a spirit that would not be crushed. Imagine Trinity being forced to marry. It would never happen.

'You wouldn't do that to Layla,' Zahid said, but the king nodded for Abdul to leave them for a moment and, once alone, he addressed his son.

'Today there are reports in the news that I have lost weight. Last week it was reported that during my last overseas trip I was hospitalised. Soon I will not be well enough to leave Ishla for my treatments and the people will know that I have little time left. They need to know the future is secure.' It was said without emotion and should be accepted the same way. Feelings were frowned upon, especially for a male royal, but Zahid could not allow Layla to be used as a pawn. If he married then he could change things for Layla, who, unlike him, believed in foolish things like a marriage based on love.

It was not just the king that Layla had wrapped around her little finger. History meant that Zahid too, was extremely protective towards his sister. Not that Layla knew why, for the time of the queen's death and its aftermath must never be discussed.

'I want to announce a royal wedding,' the king reiterated. 'I want to hear cheering in the street when you walk onto the balcony with your chosen bride.'

'Chosen?' Zahid's word was tart. For all the dining with families that would take place, for all the pomp and ceremony that went in to choosing a bride, both the king and Zahid knew it was a given. Zahid must choose Princess Sameena of Bishram and right his father's wrongs for Fahid had not chosen wisely.

Instead of choosing Princess Raina of Bishram, a younger Fahid had fallen in love.

Zahid though, would choose wisely. Sameena

was his father's first choice, for the long-ago snub to the now Queen Raina still caused problems and both men hoped for friendlier relations between Ishla and Bishram.

Zahid, though, leaned towards Sheikha Kumu.

Her country, though small, was prosperous and had an extremely efficient army.

It was a business decision to Zahid and one he would not take lightly.

'You do not need to ask the Fayeds to dine just yet.' Finally Zahid relented. 'You are right: the people have already waited long enough for their prince to choose his bride. Six months to a year sounds a suitable time frame.'

'I am pleased to hear it,' the king said, and then called his aide to join them again. 'Abdul, do what is necessary for the renovations to commence.' He did little to contain the smile of victory that played on his lips as he continued speaking. 'And send out the invitations for potential brides and their families to dine.'

Zahid walked through to the master suite and on the king's instruction a servant opened the huge shutter and the sun streamed into the room and fell on a large carved wooden bed. Here, Zahid and his bride would first live till, on the king's death, they moved to the first palace to rule the land that he loved.

Zahid did not have six months left to enjoy being single for once his bride was officially chosen his playboy reputation must become a thing of the past.

It was a very sobering thought and one that did not go unnoticed by his sister.

As he prepared to fly to London for Donald's wedding, Layla came to his suite.

'Father says that the renovations are starting.'

'Correct.'

'Do you know who you will choose as your bride?'

Zahid did not answer, not that Layla let that stop the conversation.

'Perhaps Sheikha Kumu?' Layla fished. 'She is well connected and very pretty, or maybe Princess Sameena, she's so beautiful—'

'It is not about looks,' Zahid interrupted. 'I

will choose the bride who will best serve our people. One who will understand that my heart belongs to them.'

Layla rolled her eyes. 'Ah, but I bet you take looks into consideration when you are choosing your lovers.'

'Layla!' Zahid warned, but she would not quiet.

'Why don't women get to go overseas? Why were you allowed to leave Ishla for your education?'

'You know why, Layla.'

'Well, it's not fair. At least you have had some fun before you choose your bride. Father is speaking about the Fayeds again. I don't want Hassain to be my first love.' She pulled a face and Zahid suppressed a smile. He wanted to tell his sister that when he was king he would change things, but that conversation was too dangerous to have just yet.

'I want to know what it is to fall in love.' Layla pouted.

Zahid could think of nothing worse than a

mind dizzied by emotion. He truly could not stand the thought of a life lived in love.

Yes, there was a year of her life that Layla didn't know about.

The first year.

He looked at his sister who lived with her head in the clouds, yet he cared for her so. He could still remember her screaming in the crib, could still recall their father's repeated rejection of his second born, who he had blamed for his wife's death.

No, Layla must never know.

'Layla, the palace will be busy preparing for my wedding. You do not have to worry for a while.'

'But I do worry,' Layla said. 'Zahid, can I come to England with you? I would love to see the sights, and to go to a real English wedding...'

'Layla, you know that you cannot travel until you are married.'

'No,' Layla corrected him, 'the rule is that I cannot travel unless I am escorted by a family member. If you took me...'

'I am not taking you to England with me,' Zahid said. He would already have his work cut out with the Fosters and their debauched ways, let alone adding Layla to the mix. Zahid rolled his eyes. There was no doubt in his mind that his best-man duties would involve policing Trinity.

Once he had agreed to attend the wedding, Zahid had looked her up and his face had hardened as he had read on and flicked through images. Having completed school, or rather, as Zahid knew from Donald, a stint in rehab, Trinity had, it would seem, jumped straight off the wagon. There were several pieces about how she loved to party, combined with several images of her falling out of nightclubs. Things had gone quiet in recent years, though. She was now living in California and only came home on occasion, such as for the wedding of her brother.

His curiosity about Trinity surprised even Zahid. He could barely remember most of the women he had dated, yet the one kiss that he and Trinity had shared still remained clear in his mind, so much so that it took a moment to drag his mind back to the conversation.

'Can I come on your honeymoon, then?' Layla persisted.

'I will hopefully be busy on my honeymoon,' Zahid said.

'Not the desert part.' Layla laughed. 'After. When you travel overseas, can I at least come with you then?'

It was not such a strange request—sisters often travelled as companionship for the new bride.

'You might not like the bride I choose,' Zahid pointed out.

'*You* might not like the bride you choose.' Layla smiled. 'So I will entertain her so that you do not have to worry about such things as shopping and lunch.'

'We shall see.'

'Promise me that you will take me, Zahid,' Layla said. 'I need something to look forward to.'

'You are up to something?'

'No,' Layla said. 'I am just bored and I want something to dream about, something to look forward to.' She glanced at the clock. 'I need to go and meet my students.'

'Then go,' Zahid said, but Layla would not move till she got her way.

'How can I teach my students about the world when I have never even left Ishla?'

Zahid accepted that she made a good point. 'Very well, you can travel overseas with us when I take my bride on honeymoon.'

It was no big deal to Zahid.

Romance was not part of the equation in any marriage that he had in mind and that was the reason he said yes.

CHAPTER TWO

AN ASH CLOUD, perchance? Trinity's heart lurched in hope when she saw that her flight was delayed.

A really, really big ash cloud that would ground aviation for days.

Or maybe the baggage handlers could go on strike.

LAX had been busy, busy and JFK was much the same. Trinity knew she had been cutting it almost impossibly fine to get back in time for her brother's wedding and now that her flight had been delayed there was a very real prospect that the bridesmaid wouldn't make it to the church on time.

Had she been willing that ash cloud to appear perhaps?

Of course she had.

Just a nice natural disaster where no one got

hurt and one where it could be explained in the speeches that, though Trinity had done everything she possibly could to get there…

Boarding.

Trinity watched as the sign flicked over and dragged herself to the back of the line. Even as she took her seat on the aircraft she was hoping for a black miracle.

A flock of seagulls perhaps?

Yes, an aborted take-off seemed preferable to facing her family, or rather her aunt and her husband.

When Donald had called Trinity to tell her that he was marrying Yvette, though she had given her congratulations and said that, of course, she'd be thrilled to be there, inside her stomach had churned.

On concluding the call, Trinity had actually dashed to the toilet to be sick.

She felt sick now.

A harried mother and baby took the seat next to her.

Why, oh, why, hadn't she used the money her

father had given her to buy a business-class seat, Trinity thought as the baby told her with his big blue eyes that he was going to do everything in his power to scream all the way to Heathrow.

The take-off was impeccable, not a seagull to be found!

Then the captain came on and said that he would do his level best to make up lost time.

Trinity wished she could do the same—that she could push a few buttons and ride a tail wind if it meant that she could erase lost years. An ancient art history degree that she'd somehow obtained, as she'd struggled merely to operate, lay unused. Clubs, bars, dancing had been but a temporary escape from her pain and grief. California healing had beckoned, but neither reiki, nor chakra cleansing, nor the roar of the vast Pacific could replace what had been lost.

Her latest attempt to cure her repulsion to anything that hinted on sexual had been positive-reinforcement-based training.

Ha-ha.

Two thousand dollars later and several pounds heavier, Trinity had decided that no amount of chocolate or affirmations were going to cure her particular problem.

She loved herself?

Most of the time, yes.

She'd just prefer not to be touched.

The meals were served and Trinity just picked at hers and refused wine. Despite what the newspapers said, she really only drank at family things.

Which it soon would be.

No.

As the cabin lights were dimmed Trinity tried to doze but Harry, as it turned out the baby was called, had decided now that he liked her. He kept patting her cheeks with his little fat hands.

'Sorry,' his mum kept saying.

'It's not a problem.'

Trinity tried to doze some more.

It didn't work.

The only consolation to attending the wedding was that she had just found out that, though at first he had declined, Zahid was going to be the best man.

She hadn't seen him since that night ten years ago and Trinity wondered what he would be like now, if he even remembered that kiss in the woods.

If he'd ever given her a thought since then.

Trinity closed her eyes and briefly returned to the rapture of being in his arms and the bliss of his kiss, but her eyes suddenly snapped open for she could not even escape to the sanctuary of them without recalling what had happened later that night and in the months that had followed.

There was so much adrenaline in her legs that Trinity tried walking around the sleepy cabin, dreading what she must face later today. How she'd hoped her mother would tell her that Clive and Elaine hadn't been invited, how she wished her father, or even her brother, would step in.

No one ever had.

Skeletons belonged in the closet. Dirty laundry belonged in a basket.

Clive was more prominent than her father.

Nothing could be gained by speaking out. It was easier to simply smile for the cameras.

It wasn't, though.

All too soon the scent of breakfast came from the galley and, opening the shutter, she saw dawn.

The wedding day was here.

Trinity returned to her seat, where Harry was shrieking. 'Would you mind?' his mum asked. 'I have to go to the restroom.'

'Of course.'

Trinity held Harry, who stood on her thighs with his knees buckling as he screamed and screamed. 'Go, Harry!' Trinity smiled. Wouldn't it be lovely to be as uninhibited as Harry, to simply scream out your pain and not care a jot what others thought?

She didn't get to hold babies much. All her family was in the UK and none of her friends in LA had babies yet.

The sting of tears in her own eyes was terribly unwelcome and Trinity swallowed them back, telling herself she was being ridiculous. There was no comparison, Trinity told herself as she looked at Harry.

He was all big and chunky and wriggling.

Whereas *she* had been so tiny and so very still.

The sob that escaped Trinity's lips came from somewhere so deep and buried that even Harry stopped his tirade.

'It's okay.' Trinity fought to quickly compose herself and smiled into his curious eyes as he patted her cheek. 'I'm fine.'

Trinity had no choice but to be fine.

She just missed her baby so.

Ached for the time that her daughter had never had.

'Thanks so much.' Harry's mum was back and Trinity handed him to her but the bubble of panic was rising inside her and Trinity truly did not know if she could get through today.

She pressed her bell.

'Breakfast won't be a moment.' The steward smiled.

'I'd like a bourbon, please,' Trinity said. 'A large one.'

A few minutes later the steward returned with two tiny bottles of bourbon and a pussycat smile that told Trinity she was a lush.

Trinity didn't care.

At least it calmed her enough to get off the plane.

'Where the hell is Trinity?' Donald demanded, as he clicked off his phone. 'Yvette's in tears, there's not a sign of her at the hotel…'

Here we go again! Zahid thought as he felt the pull of the mad Fosters' vortex. A night out last night with Donald and co. and Zahid was remembering all too well why he chose only minimal contact. Gus had kept insisting that Zahid extend his visit, or come and stay later in the year, and Zahid had reluctantly explained that he would be marrying soon and his time was now to be spent in Ishla.

And now, it would seem, Trinity had gone missing in action again.

Nothing changed.

'Why don't I call Dianne and see if there's an update?' Zahid suggested, for it was the best man's duty to keep the groom calm, but he had never seen Donald so tense. He made the call and then gave Donald the news. 'Your mother's at the airport and she says Trinity's plane just landed. As soon as she is through customs, she will take her straight to the hotel and help her to get ready. Call Yvette and tell her that she can stop worrying.'

'You can never stop worrying when Trinity's around!' Donald challenged. 'I just hope she's sober.'

It wasn't Donald's comment that had a certain disquiet stir in Zahid. It was his reaction to the news that Trinity had landed and that soon he would see her again.

Over the years there had been a few near misses. Zahid, when he had heard Trinity's plane was delayed, had assumed that this would be another. But that she was in the same country now brought a strange sense of calm—the planets seemed more neatly aligned, the stars just a little less random. They were in the same country and finally, after all this time, they would see each other again.

He wondered if she would be bringing someone and briefly wrestled with the distaste of that thought but then dismissed its significance. It had nothing to do with feelings, Zahid quickly told himself. After all, it was possibly his last weekend in England as a single man and certainly there was unfinished business between them. It was natural to be hoping that she was attending the wedding alone.

Trinity didn't have to wait for baggage and she raced out of customs, her heart aflutter. Despite everything, she was looking forward to seeing her mum. Maybe things would be different now, Trinity hoped as her eyes scanned the crowd for Dianne. Maybe her mum would realise just how difficult today was. Maybe…

Her heart lurched in hope as she saw her mum, dressed for the wedding, just minus a hat. Trinity raced over and gave her a hug. 'I'm so sorry.'

'Have you been drinking?' was Dianne's only response to her daughter's kiss.

'I had one bourbon on the plane.'

'It's whisky,' Dianne hissed. 'You're in England now. Where the hell have you been?'

'The plane was delayed.'

'I don't want to hear your excuses.'

Trinity could feel her mother's fingers digging into her arms as they raced to get a taxi and Dianne didn't let up as they sped to the hotel. 'Yvette is in tears. She wanted her own sister to be bridesmaid and now you've made us look...' Dianne struggled to contain her temper. It had taken many, many dinners to convince Yvette's parents to choose Trinity for the role, but a generous helping hand towards the wedding bill had given them leverage and the Fosters had insisted that their voice be heard.

Oh, and so too would Trinity's voice be heard, Dianne remembered. She just had to tell Trinity that! 'I've told Yvette that you're going to sing near the end of the night.'

'Excuse me.' Trinity's mouth was agape. 'I can't sing.'

'You've got a beautiful voice.'

'Actually, I don't.' Trinity could not believe that they'd ask this of her. 'Mum, please, I don't want to sing. I just want to...'

Hide.

'When do you go back?' Dianne asked.

'Tomorrow afternoon.'

'So it really is a flying visit, then.'

'I've got an interview next week.'

'If you'd let your father help, you wouldn't be out of work.'

'I'm not out of work,' Trinity bristled, because she had a job at the beach bar and she certainly earned her money there, but Dianne pulled a face.

'If anyone asks, say...' Dianne thought for a moment. 'Say you're working in a museum.'

'You want me to lie?'

'Yes, please!' Dianne said. 'We didn't put you

through an art history degree to have you working in a bar.'

'Ancient art,' Trinity corrected, and then smirked at her mum. 'What sort of museum exactly?' She watched as her mother's neck went red.

'Okay, a library, then. The reference section. At one of the big colleges.'

Nothing changed.

They got to the hotel and the shoebox of a room that had been booked for Trinity. After a lightning-quick shower she sat as her hair was brushed and coiled and pinned by her tense mother while Trinity quickly did her make-up. Moods weren't improved when her mother unzipped a bag and pulled out the most awful blue dress that Trinity had ever seen.

'You are joking?' Trinity said. 'It's so shiny I'm going to need sunglasses to wear it.'

'Had you bothered to come to any of the fittings then you might have had a say in what you were wearing. As it is…' She lifted up Trinity's arm and attempted to pull up the concealed zip that was located at the side. 'You've put on weight!' Dianne accused.

'No,' Trinity said. 'I gave you my measurements exactly.'

'Then why can't I do it up?'

Because you refused to believe I was ten pounds heavier than your goal weight for me, Trinity thought, but said nothing, just sucked in her stomach and chest as her mother tugged at the stupid zip until finally it was up.

'Is breathing an optional extra?' Trinity quipped.

'Yes,' Dianne snapped back. 'But smiling isn't. This is your brother's day.'

'Oh, funny, that, I thought it was Yvette's.'

'Trinity!' Dianne was struggling to hold onto her temper. 'Don't start.'

'I'm not starting anything, I was just saying…'

'Well, don't!' Dianne warned. 'You've already done your level best to ruin this day. All you have to do now is smile. Can you manage that?''

'Of course, but I'm not singing.'

'And lose the smart mouth.' Dianne secured

her hat as she issued instructions. 'Go now and apologise to Yvette. I'm going to make my way to the church. I'll see you there and I'm warning you...'

'Noted.'

'I mean it, Trinity, I don't want a scene from you today.'

She should say nothing, Trinity knew that. She should just nod and reassure her mum that she'd behave, but, hell, she had a voice and as much as her parents loathed that fact, Trinity was determined to find it.

'Then just make sure I'm not put in any position where I might need to make a scene,' Trinity said, and her mother's silk-clad shoulders stiffened and Trinity watched as the feather sticking out of Dianne's hat shivered in anger as Trinity refused to comply with orders.

'Will you just...?' Dianne hissed, and turned around. 'Can you try and remember that this is your brother's wedding and not spoil a family gathering for once.' Her face was right up at Trinity's. 'For once can today not be about you?'

'Of course.' Trinity stared back coolly but her heart was hammering in her chest. 'Just make sure that you keep that sleaze well away from me.'

'Are you still going on about that? It was years ago...' Two champagnes on an empty stomach that was fluttering with mother-of-the-groom nerves and Dianne would not be argued with, and certainly she wanted nothing to spoil what *had* to be a perfect day. 'You will behave, Trinity, you will be polite and you will smile.'

It had been stupid to hope things might be different.

Nothing had changed, Trinity realised.

Nothing ever would.

'What are you doing?' Trinity asked, as she watched her mother's painfully slow attempt to write a text. 'I'll do it.'

'It's done,' Dianne said, as her phone made the small whooshing sound that meant her text had been sent. 'I was just letting Zahid know that you're on your way to Yvette and that everything's back on schedule.'

As she took the elevator to Yvette's room for the first time that morning Trinity smiled.

As he pulled his phone from his pocket and read the text, so too did Zahid.

CHAPTER THREE

IT WAS NOT the bride who drew Zahid's eye as she entered the church; instead, it was the woman who walked behind her who held his attention.

There was a smile fixed on Trinity's face but her eyes were as wary and as truculent as the teenage Trinity's, but then they met his and Zahid watched as her pale cheeks infused with pink. For both of them there was a moment's return to a wood many years ago and a kiss that both wished had drawn to a more natural conclusion.

Zahid smiled, which he rarely did, and Trinity was so lost for a moment, so taken aback by Zahid's smile that as the bride halted, for a second Trinity didn't. She actually forgot her place, for it was as if she should simply walk on to Zahid—to go now and greet him as her body wanted to and wrap her arms around his neck, but instead, after a brief falter, Trinity halted and took the flowers from Yvette.

Zahid turned his back to her then and the service commenced.

The service was long, not by Zahid's standards, just terribly long to stand there and not turn around when he would have preferred to.

Though Zahid stared ahead, he was looking at her very closely in his mind and re-examining the Trinity he'd seen today.

Her dress was terrible. Like a synthetic sapphire, it lacked depth and mystery and it was far too tight. Her hair was worn up and dotted with violets that matched the dark smudges under her eyes, yet she looked, to Zahid, amazing. Sunkissed, dirty blonde, fragile and sexy, she was everything he remembered her to be and more.

Trinity stared ahead, loathing that her shoulders were bare and wondering whose eyes were on them. She hated the loud sound of her aunt's husband singing a hymn, as if he meant the words, as if he were a decent man.

So, instead of dwelling on the man behind and to the right, she fixed her gaze ahead and stared at Zahid, a man who did not know the words but neither did Zahid pretend to sing. He stood firm and dignified and she willed him to turn around.

He didn't.

He could have no idea the torture today was for her, for she could tell no one about her past— that had been spelt out to her many years ago. His raven hair was glossy and immaculate, his shoulders wider than before and possibly he was taller. She saw the clenching of his fist in the small of his back and remembered that same hand on her waist when the world had seemed so straightforward. As he handed over the rings she was treated to a glimpse of his strong pro-file and her ears strained to capture whatever words he murmured to Donald.

Zahid was as conscious of Trinity as she was of him, so much so that as they all squeezed into the vestry for the signing of the register, despite the chatter from others, he only heard her exhale in brief relief.

'Trinity…' her father warned as she leant against the wall to catch her breath, so relieved was she to be away from Clive.

Donald and Yvette signed the register and Gus added his signature with a flourish. Trinity watched as Zahid added his. *Sheik Prince Zahid Bin Ahmed of Ishla.*

'Leave some space for me.' Trinity smiled and then added her own signature.

Trinity Natalii Foster.

Her hand was shaking, Trinity realised as she put down the pen, only the nerves she had now felt very different to the ones that she'd had before.

As she stepped back from the register she caught the deliciously familiar scent of Zahid and as he lowered his head to her ear the tiny bones all shivered awake to the deep, long-buried thrill of his low, intimate voice.

'Natalii?'

'Born at Christmas,' Trinity said. 'Please never repeat it again, I hate it.'

Of course she had been born at Christmas, Zahid thought, for, unbeknown to Trinity he had returned to the Fosters' in the hope of seeing her in the new year after she would have turned eighteen.

Trinity hadn't been there.

She was here now, though, and Zahid spoke on.

'I thought that it was the bride's prerogative to be late.'

'You know how I loathe tradition.'

'Does that mean we shan't be dancing later?' Zahid asked, and she turned to his slow smile. 'Given how you loathe tradition.'

Oh!

Trinity blinked for it was as if he didn't know she was dead inside, as if he didn't know that her frigid body no longer worked, yet it felt now as if it did, for a pulse was working high in her neck—Trinity could feel it, and her stomach was fluttering as it had years before on that night.

With Zahid beside her, she could remember the beauty, rather than dwell on the pain.

'I suppose we shall...' Trinity sighed, as if dancing with Zahid would be a huge concession. 'I'd hate to cause trouble.'

'Liar,' Zahid said, and his hand met the small of her back as he guided her out of the vestry.

With one brief exchange, with that small touch, she was back in the woods, innocent and unfurling to his hand, and it was actually dizzying to walk behind Yvette and Donald and through the congregation. More than that, it was exhilarating to step outside into the sun and, on the day Trinity had been dreading, she felt her heart soaring like the bells that rang out around them.

To be, for the first time, at such a function and be just a little bit taken care of, for Zahid's duty now was not just to the groom, was, to Trinity, amazing.

He stood for the wedding photos and even

made the unbearable a touch less so as the family all gathered around.

'Smile, Trinity,' he said out of the corner of his mouth, and she forgot the shiver of dread that Clive was near.

'You don't,' she pointed out, and then frowned at her own words because Zahid smiled so readily when their eyes met and held.

'It is not in my nature to smile.'

For some reason that made her giggle just enough for the photographer to get his shot and then they piled into cars and they met at the hotel.

As the bride and groom entered, one look at her very relaxed brother and Trinity knew that Donald must be on something.

Please, no, Trinity begged in her head.

He had promised her he was over that now.

She and Zahid sat at opposite ends of the top table and though she wished they were sitting next to each other, maybe it was for the best, Trinity thought, for just knowing he was here was distracting enough.

Anyway, they'd no doubt run out of conversation within two minutes, though she was dying to know what he was up to and desperate to know if he was seeing someone.

Surely not, Trinity consoled herself, because back in the vestry Zahid had definitely been flirting.

She struggled through the meal, her reward that awaited her dance with him, and soon enough it was time for the speeches.

To his credit, Zahid did unbend a fraction and asked for some sparkling water for the toasts!

God, he was so controlled, so well behaved, Trinity thought, stretching her legs under the table and slipping off her shoes as the speeches started and doing her best not to yawn, not because she was bored by the speeches but because jet-lag was starting to seriously hit.

Yvette's father went first, thanking everyone and saying how thrilled he was to welcome Donald into the family. Zahid's face was impassive but he privately thought that Yvette's father had the look of a man who had brought home a puppy for the children only to realise it was going to grow into the size of a small horse.

It was the small horse's turn next and Zahid watched as Yvette scratched anxiously at her neck as her very new husband took to his feet.

Donald thanked everyone too, especially his beautiful wife. 'I'd like to thank Zahid for all his help and for travelling so far to be here.' Donald smiled a loaded smile. 'You've been an excellent best man and I hope to return the favour when it is your turn to marry next year.'

Zahid's jaw clamped down as Donald rambled on and he glanced over at Trinity. Her cheeks were red, an angry red, and she was dribbling salt on her sorbet.

He hadn't wanted her to hear his news like that.

As Donald proposed a toast to the bridesmaids, Zahid watched as Trinity raised her glass…

But to a passing waiter.

Oh, Trinity.

He wanted to go over and halt her, to whisk her away, to explain that she had misunderstood.

It was the truth, though.

And this early in the evening the truth hurt them both.

Zahid duly stood and thanked the groom for his words on behalf of the bridesmaids, though privately he'd have liked to knock him out. Then he thanked everyone else that he had to and said all the things that a best man should, but then it came to the part where Donald should star, where this future king should demure and ensure that the groom shone.

'Donald and I...' Zahid glanced at his notes and then faltered, and Trinity looked up at the brief hesitation as Zahid silently recalled a teenage incident and saw it now through the eyes of a man.

They were your drugs.

He could see it so clearly now and yet here he stood, all these years later, paying the price for Donald's supposed valour.

Well, no more.

'Donald and I...' Zahid resumed his speech but he was not looking at his notes now '...attended the same school and later were students at the same university.' Trinity heard her father's cough in an attempt to prompt Zahid, and she looked at her brother's expectant face, but the glory never came. Zahid went on to recall a few antidotes and all in all it was a very nice speech—he just forgot to paint Donald as the hero in Zahid's life.

False duty had been more than repaid.

And so to the dancing.

Zahid stood over Trinity, waiting for her to join him on the floor, but it was a touch more complicated than standing for Trinity, because her already tight shoes refused to go back on, but finally she forced her feet into them. 'The things I do for my family,' Trinity said, as he led her to the floor. 'Not that they appreciate it.'

'I am appreciative...' Zahid said, as he loosely held her and they started to dance and she waited for him to finish his sentence.

He didn't.

'Of what?' Trinity prompted. 'You are appreciative of what?'

'That you are here,' Zahid said. 'That we see each other again after all this time.'

They both knew it was running out for them and there was no tail wind to help them catch up, no buttons to push that could change things.

Except he pushed the right ones.

Zahid was the only man who did.

'I loved your speech,' Trinity said, her words a little stilted, for she was cross with Zahid for flirting when he was about to be wed. Yet she was cross only from the neck up. Her body had seemed to overlook the fact he would soon be marrying the very second that she was in his arms.

'You're the only one who liked it. Your father looks as if he wants to kill me.'

'It's me he's shooting daggers at!' Trinity looked to the right and smiled sweetly at her father. 'I was late, you know?'

'You were.'

'And not looking out for my brother.'

Zahid looked down to those blue eyes again and wondered how much she knew, for he was sure that Donald was high. 'Is it nice to see your brother happy?'

'Donald wouldn't know what happy was if it was hand delivered and he had to sign for it.' She looked over at Donald, who was smiling and laughing to his bride. 'He's loaded,' Trinity said. 'Nothing changes.'

'You?' Zahid said.

'I don't go near anything like that.'

'I meant,' Zahid corrected himself, 'are you happy?'

'Not today,' Trinity said, then it was she who corrected herself. 'Actually, right now I am.'

'Because?'

'Because,' Trinity said, because in his arms she actually was and, no, she should not be flirting, she had been called a tease so very many times when she was unable to follow through, but she just needed one lovely thing to focus on, just the teeniest bit of help to get through the night and, for good or bad, Zahid was it.

'Because?' he said into her ear, and it was then that she succumbed.

'Because my brother has excellent taste in groomsmen.'

'His bride has terrible taste in dresses.'

'She does,' Trinity sighed. 'Though in fairness my mother would have lied about my measurements. She prefers me with an eating disorder, it makes her a more visible martyr...'

Trinity was, Zahid decided, rather wise.

'I'm supposed to be singing later,' Trinity said, and her hands moved up and linked behind his neck and, yes, they were back in the woods again. 'As I said to my mother, my name isn't Trinity Von Trapp.' She went to explain, because he probably had no idea what she was talking about, but then she remembered a long-ago Christmas and Dianne forcing them to watch the *Sound of Music* and Trinity giggling at Zahid's somewhat bemused expression.

More than that, though, somehow he got

her—she did not have to explain everything to Zahid.

'Rolfe might join you,' he said into her ear, and though Zahid would no more sing than fly to the moon a smile played on her lips as she pulled her head back, just enough that her back arched in just a little and Zahid's tongue rolled to his cheek as something else stirred to her words.

'I prefer the captain.'

It was a tiny dirty dance, but with words. The heat from his palms was surely searing her dress and the way he simply let her be had her breathing freely for the first time since she could remember. With Zahid her body seemed to know how to work. He induced only pleasure and made it safe to be a touch wanton.

Then she remembered she was cross with him.

As the music ended, instead of sinking in for another dance, she pulled back.

'I'd better go and see how Yvette is.'

'I will check on the groom.' He gave a small nod. 'Perhaps later we dance…'

Trinity gave a tight smile as she walked off but she felt conflicted. No doubt Zahid thought her a party girl, no doubt he assumed where the night was leading.

He could never guess that she felt ill at the very thought of sex.

Only she didn't feel ill in his arms.

Trinity wanted to get back to him, only Yvette was teary and she either had raging cystitis or her bladder was the size of a thimble or more likely she really was pregnant, because she wanted to go to the loo on the hour every hour and Trinity had to help with the dress.

'Your brother…' Yvette was trying to tame her angry cheeks with Trinity's foundation. 'I just got a call from the hotel—he hasn't paid the reservation fee…'

'I'm sure it's just a mix-up,' Trinity suitably soothed.

She was quite sure to the contrary, though.

The night wore on and the only time they met

was when Dianne introduced Trinity to a group that Zahid was in and, of course, one of them had to ask what she was doing with her degree.

'I'm thinking of moving to France.' Trinity beamed, deciding that it might not be such a bad idea actually and feeling her mother's tension beside her, 'but right now I work in a library at a large college—'

'The reference section,' Dianne interrupted, and Zahid watched the daggers that shot from Trinity's eyes.

Dianne was determined that Trinity would sing and trying to escape the inevitable, true to form, Trinity slipped outside for some air.

Zahid wasn't faring much better. All night Donald insisted on introducing him to everyone as his best friend from way back and slapping Zahid on the back as he did so.

It came as no surprise when Donald pulled Zahid aside near the end of the night and asked if he might have a word.

'I know that you're flying back after lunch

tomorrow and that we might not get another chance to speak,' Donald said.

'You don't have to entertain me on your wedding night.' Zahid tried to smile, tried to keep things light, tried not to like this man any less than he now did.

'And I know that you've always been a great friend to me, as I hope I have to you.' *They were your drugs,* Zahid said again in his head, but he remained silent as Donald spoke on. 'The thing is, Zahid…' And Zahid listened as, again, Donald asked him to help—that if he could just take care of the honeymoon, then as soon as Donald was back he would repay him.

'I am not paying for your honeymoon.' Zahid interrupted the familiar tirade but with its latest twist. 'What I will pay for is three months of rehabilitation.'

'That's really generous but if I could just get these debts paid then I wouldn't need rehab. All I'm asking—'

'I have told you what I am prepared to do. I

have heard of a good clinic near Texas. A family friend had their son go there...'

'I've just got married I can hardly disappear on Yvette...'

'I would say that you have been absent from your relationship for quite some time,' Zahid said, refusing to be swayed. It was clear from looking at Yvette that Donald would soon be a father—it was time, then, that he grew up. 'If you go to rehab, I will take care of your debts.'

'Zahid, please, can you just—?'

'No.'

Zahid refused to negotiate.

'I will speak with the accounting firm that I use in the UK. The offer is there so long as you are prepared to meet my conditions.'

'You can afford to help me out without blinking.'

'That has nothing to do with it. Even if I had no money but you were determined to change, I would take a loan to pay for your treatment. I will not be used. You can work for a better life, or you can torch what you have. You choose.'

'Some friend!' Donald sneered.

Zahid stepped away from Donald and headed outside just as he heard Dianne start up with the familiar cry. 'Has anyone seen Trinity?'

Zahid was looking at her now.

She was a *bad* bridesmaid, if there was such a thing. The flowers were wilting in her hair as she drained her champagne glass and then muttered something very unladylike under her breath.

'Language, Trinity,' Zahid said, and she rolled her eyes.

'I hate weddings.'

'They are a part of life.'

'Well, if I ever get married it will be on a beach with no guests.' She glanced at him. 'What about you?'

'There will be many guests and it will go for two or three days. It will be a national holiday and the wedding date will be marked each year with the same…'

It sounded so horrific to Trinity that she actually laughed. 'I shouldn't complain really. So—'

Trinity tried to keep her voice light '—when is your wedding day?'

'I will marry next year.'

It was ridiculous, Trinity thought, but as she stood there she was filled with a strange ache of sadness.

One kiss might not sound much, but that one kiss was her only pleasant memory even remotely attached to sex.

'You ought to go back inside,' Zahid said. 'Your mother is looking for you.'

'I loathe them,' Trinity said.

'It shows.'

'I love them, though.' He was surprised by her admission, not that she loved her family, more at the hopelessness in her voice. 'Do you get on with your family?'

'I do,' Zahid said. 'Most of the time.'

'Meaning?'

'Meaning most of the time I get on with them.'

'You're terribly straightforward.'

'Meaning?'

'Just that.'

'You should never assume,' Zahid said, for his thoughts were less than straightforward where Trinity was concerned.

'I don't want to go back in,' Trinity admitted. 'Do you think anyone would really notice if I just disappeared?'

'You know that they would,' Zahid said. 'It will only go for another half-hour or so.'

She let out a breath. Half an hour felt like an eternity right now. 'I don't want to sing.'

'There are many things that I would prefer not to do.'

'But you do them.'

'Some of the time.'

'Would you sing?'

God, but she loved it when he smiled.

'No.'

His smile almost turned to a wince as Dianne's voice invaded them again. 'Trinity?'

He watched her jaw grit as the call continued and her mother's voice started to get near. Zahid took Trinity's arm and led her around the corner to where it was dark, and she could smell the pine from a tree and the thud of music and people in the distance and she wished they were back there in the woods.

'I wish you'd taken me with you that night.'

'I was tempted.'

'It didn't show,' Trinity said, and in sudden defence she mocked him a little. 'Have you been trained to hide your emotions?'

'Who said that I had any?'

She attempted a suitable reply but it dawned then that his hand was on her waist and the other was on her face when normally contact, any contact, was unbearable, just not tonight, and so she answered his question. 'Your kiss told me that you did.'

'Sex is not an emotion,' came his brusque response, but for the first time he lied and she knew it, for neither could deny what thrummed between them now. It was more than lust yet it tasted almost the same, it was more than want yet still he fought not to call it need as he looked to her lips.

'Where were we?' Zahid asked, but the years

could not disappear. There was so much hurt there that for Trinity it was not as simple as a kiss. So great was her fear of contact she was petrified how she might react to his touch. She knew about his reputation with women and, of course, he assumed hers, but just as a kiss was surely inevitable Trinity saw her way out and she leapt on it and wriggled from his arms. 'I doubt your fiancée would be very pleased…'

'I have not chosen my bride yet,' Zahid said, and he took her champagne glass and placed it on a window ledge then pulled her back to where she had been just a second or two ago. 'If I had, I would not be about to kiss you.'

'Oh.'

Well, that settled that, then, Trinity thought. There was nothing to stop them other than her fear and that she could not stand being held by a man, except she was being held now and there was no urge to run, there was no urge to do anything other than receive the lips softly descending on hers.

Would he be able to tell from her kiss, her terror? Trinity wondered.

No, she fast realised, because to his mouth there was no terror, just the melting of fear and the bliss of his lips and the stroke of his tongue.

Would he be able to tell from her rigid body that she did not know how to respond, that her body refused to obey?

No, because she sank into his embrace without thought and the press of his erection against her felt like a reward.

His mouth *did* make the pain disappear; his kiss did, on a night she had been dreading, actually allow her to forget, and Trinity found out something new—it was very hard to kiss and smile at the same time but she was trying.

'What are you doing?' Zahid said, as she paused for a moment and allowed her mouth to stretch into the beam that this moment deserved.

'Smiling,' Trinity said. 'That's better.' For her lips could better relax against his now.

He kissed her deeper, and Trinity felt the

weight of his mouth and the hastening of his tongue as he pulled her harder into him, she felt again the press of him on her stomach. The ugliest dress in the world fast became her favourite as his hands roamed the silk and located the not-so-stupid concealed zip and expertly slid it down just enough for his thumb to stroke her aching nipple.

The sirens were back, the sirens she'd heard but once, only they were louder now, closer now, with each and every stroke of his tongue.

Her hands were in his hair, she was back on tiptoe again but with the guide of his hand this time and the sirens neared dangerously close for both of them. She wanted him to lift her, she wanted her legs coiled around his hips. Visions of just that took over as Zahid struggled to halt her ascent, for he wanted to lift her, he wanted to be inside her but he would never compromise her.

'Not here...' Zahid pulled his mouth from her lips but they did not leave her face as she spoke.

'As I said, you deserve better than the woods. Do what you have to and then...'

She shivered at what Zahid left unsaid.

He kissed her ear and then peeled his face from hers and turned her a little. Lifting her arm, he dealt with the zip but did not leave things there. Instead, he kissed the sensitive flesh of her upper arm, and how he found her armpit sexy, she would never know, but clearly he did, because he was deep kissing her there now. Her panties were soaking. Trinity wanted to be back in his arms, but he turned her to face him and straightened her dress and then rearranged a few tendrils of her hair. 'I will be in in a moment,' Zahid said.

'Come in with me.'

'Trinity, go in.' Zahid's smile was wry for there was no way he could go back to the reception just yet. 'I'll be there soon.'

She almost floated in, just on a high from his kiss and the very real promise of tonight. Finally, finally, her body seemed to know how to respond, finally the curse was lifting.

It was possibly the very worst time to come face to face with her mother, closely followed by Clive.

'Everyone's waiting for you, Trinity,' Dianne said.

She just stood there, praying for Zahid to come up behind her, to take her hand, to just walk her away, but instead she faced this man with only the pathetic barrier of her mother between them.

'It's time to sing!' Dianne smiled.

'You want me to sing?' Trinity said, her voice a challenge.

'You know that I do.'

One moment she had been the happiest she'd ever been, Trinity realised, but now she was suddenly the angriest.

Oh, she'd sing!

Trinity was ready to sing from the treetops now!

She marched into the hall, muttering, and strode up to the microphone.

Yes, she'd sing, Trinity decided, wrenching the microphone from its stand. She'd sing as loudly as she knew how if the microphone would just stop screeching feedback.

Her starting number would be, Trinity decided, 'I Was Seventeen Going on Eighteen', and she'd point to Clive as she sang, as she told the whole world about that night.

The skeletons were coming out to play, the linen basket was going to be emptied too!

Yay!

She felt as angry and as uninhibited as Harry had been on the plane, and there was no need to hide anything, none at all.

Zahid walked into the hall in time to see Trinity stalk to the microphone and start to tap at it, tossing her hair. Her eyes spelt danger and Zahid turned as Dianne came and stood beside him. For once she wasn't wearing that plastic smile and, as everyone had this wedding day, in crisis Dianne turned to Zahid.

'Stop her!' Dianne pleaded.

Zahid wasn't following Dianne's orders as he walked to the stage, it was to get to Trinity, because there was a recklessness to her that troubled him and Zahid would not let her look a fool.

'I'd like to dedicate this number to—' Trinity started, but Zahid pulled the plug and her arm at the same time and hauled her from the stage.

'Put me down.'

'Not yet.'

'Put me down,' Trinity shouted, as he carried her over his shoulder behind the stage and out through the back exit to the elevators. It all became a little blurry then. She remembered him letting her down and Zahid demanding to know what was going on.

'Nothing!'

Jet-lag, champagne, nerves, fear, want all combined in desperate tears and then she lunged at him, desperate for escape, but Zahid denied her that. She tried to rain kisses on his face but Zahid held her at arm's length as she pecked away like an angry woodpecker who couldn't meet its mark. She wanted the sex he had promised, the bliss of escape with the one man who knew where it resided in her.

She wanted Zahid.

And so she told him.

'I don't reward bad behaviour.'

'You're not training a dolphin!' Trinity shouted, but then she started to laugh. 'I tried that, actually.' She put on an American accent. '"Positive reinforcement-based training"…and it didn't work!'

'If you want sex,' Zahid said, peeling off her dress and offloading her into the bed, 'then you can ask politely in the morning when you are sober.'

'Ask?' Trinity lay on the bed and laughed at his audacity. 'I have to ask?'

'Politely,' Zahid said. 'I want to hear the word "please" when you do,' but as he looked down at her, astonishingly, to Trinity, he smiled. 'You need to learn manners—your behaviour tonight has been shocking.'

'Really?' Trinity said. 'I thought that I'd behaved rather well.'

Zahid didn't have to come up with a suitable answer because less than ten seconds later she was sound asleep.

CHAPTER FOUR

ZAHID SAT WATCHING as Trinity started to stir.

Her bridesmaid's dress was over a chair, her shoes were on the floor, her hair was everywhere and her mascara had escaped her lashes and had moved to the pillow.

Zahid rang for breakfast and saw Trinity's eyes frown at the intrusion when a little while later the doorbell chimed.

'Just leave it there,' Zahid said, as the staff went to set up. 'Could someone draw a bath…?'

She sat up to ask everyone if they could please be quiet and get out of her room but Zahid shot her such a look that she ducked back under the covers and willed the sheikh in her bedroom to disappear.

Actually, Trinity realised, she was in his bedroom, she had to be because this room was massive and the bed seemed even bigger.

Oh, God.

As the maid came out and said that the bath had been run and Zahid said he would call soon to have the room tidied but that was all for now, Trinity had vague memories of kissing him.

Not outside, though. She remembered that that kiss had been completely lovely. It was the inside attempt to kiss him that had her cringing in recall.

'Does that groaning mean you have a recollection of last night or should I call for a doctor?'

He didn't let her hide; instead, he whipped back the bedding.

'The first one.' Trinity stared up at a very, very beautiful man. His hair was tousled and he was no longer clean-shaven and stood over her in the morning-after version of yesterday's suit.

'How is your hangover?'

'It's not a hangover, it's exhaustion,' Trinity said. 'And forty-eight hours of no sleep, mixed with champagne and my toxic family...' She closed her eyes. 'Did I make a terrible scene?'

'I brought you up here before you could,'

Zahid said, 'but, yes, you made quite a scene in the bedroom.' She could hardly breathe but then, when Zahid smiled down at her, so heart stopping was that face there was no 'hardly' about it—her breath was lodged in her lungs and it took a moment for her foggy brain to compute that Zahid wasn't cross. In fact, from the look he was giving her, any moment he'd be stripping the last of her clothing off.

Oh, God!

'Here!' He handed her a large glass of something cold and dark pink. She sat up a touch and when it met her lips, Trinity found out that it was watermelon infused with mint.

'I had no sleep on the flight. There was a baby next to me on the plane...' Trinity explained between draining her drink. 'We don't all have our own private jets to fly us to weddings...'

'You could have put on earphones.' Zahid remained unmoved by her explanations for last night's behaviour.

'You've never flown economy, have you?'

'Your father paid for business class,' Zahid

said, because he had overheard Gus telling any-one who cared to listen how much his daughter still cost him, but more than that, Zahid simply would not let her lie.

'And I bought an economy ticket with it,' Trinity whispered conspiratorially. 'It's called ten hours of discomfort for three months' rent.'

'Then you should have taken an earlier flight if you knew that you would be unlikely to get any sleep.'

She lay back on the pillow and stared at him, sulking that he wouldn't give her an out.

Yes, she should have taken an earlier flight, but that would have meant a night in the fam-ily home and it had been the last place on earth she'd wanted to be. Economy and a screaming baby had been a far more palatable option.

'Here,' Zahid said. Taking the empty glass from Trinity, he hauled her back up to a sitting position as if she were a hospital patient, and then he sat on the edge of the bed with a plate loaded with tiny sausages and pancakes. He slathered them in maple syrup and, proceeded to cut it all up and then commenced feeding her.

'I was just tired.'

'Of course you were,' Zahid said. 'Eat.'

'You're not cross?'

'No.' He smiled at her but there was concern there. 'What was going on last night?' Zahid asked. 'You were very upset when I got you back to the room.'

Trinity shrugged. 'I'd just had too much to drink.'

'That's not what you said two minutes ago.'

'I just…' Trinity shrugged. She honestly didn't know what to say.

'You can tell me.'

Could she?

He was her brother's best man, a family friend…and, right now, the very best thing in her life, even if just for a little while.

She didn't want to spoil it.

'Things get a bit tense for me when I'm with my family.'

She waited for him to tell her how wonderful her family was and that she should behave better, but Zahid was actually trying to gauge how much he should say. After all, it was her family that he was about to criticise.

He popped a forkful of food into her mouth as he chose to let his ingrained diplomacy leave him a touch, for he wanted her to hear the truth.

'I find the Fosters hard work.' As she opened her mouth to say something he reminded her that it was rude to speak with her mouth full and so Trinity had no choice but to hear him out. 'After last night, I am severing ties with your family.' As she frantically chewed so she could get her words out, Zahid beat her to it. 'When I say the Fosters I don't mean you.' Trinity stopped chewing then as Zahid spoke on—she now wanted to hear what he had to say. 'When I think of you, I do not think of the Fosters, do you understand that?'

'I think so.'

'I need you to understand that when I sever ties with you, it shall be for different reasons entirely. Do you know what they are?'

Trinity gave a tiny shrug.

'If we were to meet in the future, my feelings and thoughts about you would be very disrespectful to my future wife.' He tried to explain what Trinity could not possibly understand. 'My wife will be chosen with my country in mind.' He saw her frown break into a smile.

'I wasn't expecting her to be me.'

'I know,' Zahid said, smiling at the very thought of Trinity in Ishla. 'I'm sure you could think of nothing worse. I just want to make it very clear that when I sever ties with your family, it has nothing at all to do with how I feel about you.'

'Thank you.'

It was very nice to hear.

'And thanks for saving me from making a complete fool of myself last night,' Trinity said.

'It was no problem.'

'I was just having fun.'

His eyes said that he doubted, again, that he was hearing the truth but Trinity ploughed on regardless. In the sober light of day she certainly wasn't going to reveal the painful past and so she tried to turn the conversation to far lighter matters. 'So what does a sheikh prince do when he lets his hair down?' She stared at him for a long moment. 'I can't imagine you dancing.'

'We danced last night.'

'I mean...' She put her hands above her head and did a little dance in the bed and actually forgot she was only wearing a bra. He made her forget shame, Trinity realised as she put her arms down.

More than that, he erased it.

'I don't dance like that,' Zahid said.

'And we've established that you do sing. You don't drink?'

'No.'

'Because you're not allowed?'

'Because I don't want to.'

'Do you gamble?'

'Never.' He looked at her for a very long moment and then answered her question with one word. 'Sex.'

Trinity blinked.

'It is my vice,' Zahid said. 'We all have them.'

'Is sex a vice?'

'Apparently so.' Zahid gave a brief eye-roll. 'Though that defect will be removed soon.'

'Your wife might be a nymphomaniac,' Trinity said, and she got the lovely reward of his smile.

'We can always hope,' Zahid said, 'though it will not be something that is taken into consideration.'

'Well, it should be.' Trinity yawned.

'I shan't be raising the topic with my father.'

'We have to be down to join the family for breakfast at nine...' Trinity said, glancing at the clock and seeing that it was ten past eight as Zahid dipped the last of the pancake in syrup and offered it to her.

'You make a nice mummy bird,' Trinity said, and then duly opened her mouth, but the fork wavered there, just hovered where she couldn't reach it, and he pulled it back when she stretched her neck.

'Birds feed with their mouths,' Zahid said, and Trinity felt her insides fold in on themselves as he scalded her face with his eyes. Still she did not get that last piece of loaded, sugary pancake and her face turned to fire as he continued to speak. 'Okay,' Zahid said, 'you have two choices—breakfast with your family or we are otherwise engaged.'

'When you say otherwise engaged...'

Did he mean...?

Yes, Trinity realised as he took the last lovely bit of pancake and popped it in his own mouth, he did mean that, for his mouth was pushing her down to the pillow and he was feeding her terribly intimately now. Tongue, pancake and maple syrup were being pushed into her by his tongue and he didn't even let her close her mouth as she struggled to swallow.

It was moreish!

Filthy, messy, sticky and so very, very, nice, but as her mouth emptied and his kiss lingered on she moved her face back. 'I haven't brushed my teeth,' Trinity said, shy all of a sudden, but

Zahid seemed more than happy to accept that she might need some space.

'I am going to have a quick shower,' Zahid said, licking the last remnants of maple syrup from her mouth and then releasing her, leaving her more than a bit breathless. 'Then, if you want, you can have your bath.'

It was up to Trinity. Whatever her choice, Zahid would not be joining the Fosters at breakfast.

Duty was done.

He just hoped now that it was time for pleasure.

Zahid stood and started to unbutton his shirt. 'When I come out I will ring for someone to come and sort out the room.'

Trinity nodded, surprised that he clearly expected her to be able to speak at her first sighting of his torso. His coffee-coloured skin gleamed and his dark nipples drew her eyes, but it was the very flat stomach and the snake of dark hair beckoning downwards that had Trinity suddenly look away and start pleating the sheet with her fingers.

'I won't be long,' Zahid said, and headed to the shower as she lay back on the pillows and blew out a breath, trying and failing not to think about him sliding off his trousers and naked on the other side as she heard the taps being turned on.

He was giving her the chance to leave, Trinity realised. The chance to gather her things and go to her own room. To have breakfast with her family safe in the knowledge that this would never be mentioned again.

If she left now, she would never see him again.

Trinity lay on the bed and listened as the taps were turned off and a few moments later he came out, carrying his trousers, which he put over the chair. One white towel was around his hips, the other around his neck.

'Still here?' Zahid smiled and took the towel from his shoulders and started to dry his chest and under his arms.

'Looks like it.'

'I'll get the place sorted.'

'I'll have my bath.'

She climbed out of bed and walked to the bathroom but turned at the last moment, in time to see Zahid take off the towel from his hips. And Trinity got more of a glimpse of what she was letting herself in for. It was darker than he, thick and tumescent, and so incredibly beautiful that rather than wanting to grab her dress and run or head for the other side of the bathroom door, she actually wanted to go back to bed.

'You should call your family,' Zahid said, as if it were completely normal to be chatting to her while naked, as if it was completely normal to want the plates cleared and the place tidied and all distractions put on hold before settling in for a lovely long session.

'Er, after my bath,' Trinity croaked, for she wanted nothing to burst the fragile bubble that she carried into the bathroom with her and only released once she had closed the door. The most fragile bubble she had ever carried, for she actually wanted sex, rather than wanted to want sex.

The lighting had been turned down and the huge sunken bath was filled with warm milky-looking water.

She felt all giddy and disorientated but in the nicest way. She looked in the mirror. Her hair was a disaster, her eyes on fire and her body felt as if it was filled with helium, so floaty and high was she from pancake-laden kisses and the promise of more to come.

There was a little card telling her the infusions that her bath contained—frankincense, neroli and argan oils—and that she was to add the bomb at her leisure.

It was the bomb of bath bombs, Trinity thought as she watched it spinning in the water, tossing out petals and the most heavenly fragrances that lured her to climb in.

She lay there in the just right temperature water, with her stomach pleasantly full and her thirst more than quenched, yet for the first time, the very first time since her very first kiss with Zahid, there was a stir of want for a very different pleasure.

Zahid thought her a party girl—that a morning sex marathon was surely commonplace for her.

He'd fall off his mummy-bird perch if he knew just how limited her experience was.

Yet as she lay there, recalling his kisses and her body's response to them, it dawned on Trinity that after all those years of therapy and Californian healing, which hadn't worked a jot, the answer could well be on the other side of the door.

If Zahid had so much as a clue how messed up she was sexually then everything they had now would disappear. He'd either do the honourable thing and decline because nothing could ever come of them or, worse, she'd get pity sex, with Zahid being all careful and tender and asking if she was okay every five minutes.

Zahid wanted straightforward sex but there was nothing straightforward about sex for Trinity.

Yet she wanted Zahid to look at her the way he had this morning, she wanted the absence of fear that he brought, not just to her mind but her body too.

Still, if she was going to carry this off, then a confident, assured woman must walk out of this bathroom. Somehow she must present herself as the sexually experienced woman that he assumed she was.

'The maid has been.' Zahid knocked at the door. 'And your phone keeps buzzing. Do you want me to bring it in to you?'

'I'll be out in a minute, Zahid!' Trinity called to the closed bathroom door. 'About what you said last night…well, it would seem that I forgot to say please…' She could almost feel his smile behind the door as he answered her.

'Just remember to say thank you.'

Trinity ducked her head under the water but it didn't wipe the smile from her face. It should worry her really that the rather staid Zahid seemed to be the only person in the world who got her sense of humour. Most people frowned, or she had to explain and by then it wasn't so funny.

She didn't have to explain herself to Zahid.

Trinity looked down and saw her nipples peeking up out of the milky bathwater and she didn't understand why she was terrified but not scared.

This was all so…planned, so clinical.

No, not clinical…

Trinity blinked as she realised she had found the word she was searching for—Zahid put the sensual into consensual.

It was a very nice word to ponder as she climbed out of the bath. There were petals from the bath bomb in her hair and sticking to her skin but Trinity just wrapped herself in a robe and ran his comb through her hair.

What if she couldn't carry it off? Trinity thought. What if she started crying or broke down, or her complete inexperience told him that she hadn't a clue?

You'll *never* get a chance like this again, Trinity warned her reflection.

Kill or cure.

She opened the bathroom door, half expecting the slight chaos of this morning.

Instead, the room was in darkness, broken only by the candles dotted everywhere.

The breakfast things had been taken away, all clothes and things tidied, even the bed had that smooth freshly made look, except for the naked sheikh in it!

Trinity was terrified, of course, but nicely so, as she walked over to the bed.

'Nice bath?'

'Lovely.' She sat on the edge of the bed and wondered if the right thing to do would be to tell him but, no, as he welcomed her to his bed with a kiss, she wanted it just as it was.

His kiss made her shiver, the skill of his mouth told her to leave things to him but, just as she almost forgot to be frightened, the bleeping of her phone made her jump.

'Has anyone seen Trinity?' Zahid said, and actually made her laugh as she rose from his bed and raked her hands in frustration through wet hair. 'I'll just let them know that I won't be joining them.'

She was *far* from grateful for the reprieve— now she and Zahid would have to start all over again, Trinity thought as she picked up the phone from the bedside and read her mother's text.

'They're about to start breakfast and she wants to know where I am.' Her voice gave a little squeak at the end, because he had rolled to the side of the bed and was fiddling with the belt of her robe,

'Text and say Zahid has taken you riding.'

'Horseriding?'

'Don't lie,' Zahid said, and pulled her hips so she was standing, trying to text, as he stayed very much on his side, leaning on one elbow, one hand on her bottom, guiding her hips to his face.

It was terribly hard to text with a mouth nuzzling your stomach. She could see his glossy black hair and feel his hot mouth and tongue as she tried to work out what to write.

Oh, my, Trinity thought as he continued to kiss her stomach, because she actually wanted to drop the phone and hold his head.

Dry from her bath, she was wet from his mouth.

She wanted him lower, yet she didn't.

She wanted fear, yet it steadfastly refused to arrive.

She wanted to run, yet she wanted to remain.

Somehow she hit 'Send' on her text.

'Now turn it off.' Zahid didn't lift his mouth from her skin as he delivered far from his final instruction. 'I want no distractions.'

CHAPTER FIVE

TRINITY TURNED OFF her phone but it did not make it to the bedside table because his mouth was really working her stomach now and instead she just dropped the phone to the floor.

All phones were off, there was a 'Do not disturb' sign on the door, day had become night and all Zahid wanted to do was enjoy.

The soft skin of her stomach tasted better than even he had imagined. Still warm from the bath, it responded so readily to him. Zahid felt the tension in her stomach shifting, he felt the taut muscles relax and then tighten again, but in pleasure as his mouth moved steadily down.

Zahid was working her quickly but for one reason only—he wanted her to come.

Zahid had considered taking care of things in the shower so that he might take more time, but he had chosen to wait.

He was ruing that decision now as he deep-kissed her stomach and his hands slid up her thighs, for he had wanted Trinity for a lot longer than perhaps he cared to admit.

What to do? Trinity pondered. What should she be doing about now? Her hands moved to his hair, more to steady herself, but Zahid moved his mouth lower, nibbling at golden curls then nudging her clitoris out with his tongue as his fingers slid inside a place that no fingers had ever touched.

It was just her mind that was scared, Trinity realised, not her body, for it responded so readily to him.

She could feel a tremble in her thighs as his fingers and tongue stroked her intimately, a tremble that had her wondering if she could remain standing, but his hands soon answered that though, for he released her sex for a moment and guided her to the bed.

She thought he would kiss her, but Zahid had kissed her mouth last night and again this morning, and the first more intimate taste of her had him yearning for more and so he slid down the bed.

'Zahid…' Trinity attempted to halt him, could barely cope with her inhibition, but then came his voice.

'Do you know how many times I have thought of this?' Zahid revealed.

Why was she smiling when she should be in tears?

She could only do this with him, Trinity thought. It could only be this way, Trinity realised, for if he had seen the look of brief horror on her face at such intimate exposure, Zahid would have surely stopped.

He could not see it, though, he was too focused on her sex and guided her hips so she was kneeling over his face.

As she hovered over him his mouth kissed up her inner thigh till it met its shy mark.

'Za—' His name did role from her tongue, it halted in Trinity's throat as his tongue rolled her somewhere deep. She had meant to tell him to stop, but by the time she got to '*hid*' the world as she knew it was different.

Trinity's expression had changed from horror to a smile and then to a shocked state of bliss as all those years of frustration were swept aside by the masterful strokes of his tongue.

To him she unfolded and, though together, somehow the moment was private, the awakening exclusive to Trinity, which was how she wanted it to be, how it had to be if she wanted him to be this bold.

'I have a rose petal in my teeth,' Zahid said, though his mouth did not move away.

'They're everywhere,' Trinity breathed.

'Good,' Zahid said, returning to his heated mission. 'I find each one.'

She didn't actually have to *do* anything, Trinity realised, all she had to *do* was hold onto the bedhead and try not to moan as she followed instructions.

'Kneel lower…' Zahid breathed. 'Lower.' And she gasped as his face took more of her weight and, once it did, there was no chance of not moaning.

Unshaven, rough, wet and warm, he was everywhere that was needed, inside and out, as he devoured her with relish and his lack of inhibition gained hers.

Thank you, Trinity wanted to whimper, only not because of their earlier game—she had never been more grateful as he stirred her body beyond a simmer. She had to bite on her lip not to say it as he sucked and licked, and ran his stubbly jaw over her. His focus was so concentrated on her that Trinity didn't have to do anything other than rock to her body's tune and let out words that she would rather have kept in because they sounded so lame.

'That's lovely...' she managed. 'Lovely...' Because it was. It was as it should be and no less than that, just so nice to be lifted a little higher by his hands and his tongue kissed her more lightly, swirling her and then probing her, only pausing to tell her she was something, Trinity had no idea what, in Arabic.

'Fantastic,' Zahid translated between licks.

She felt it.

Those sirens were back and moving closer, but there was no sense of danger. She had never had an orgasm, but twice had glimpsed it with Zahid, yet she was on the very edge of one now.

'Zahid.' She said it in one word this time, for now she did want him to slow down.

'Why do you fight it?'

Because she didn't know what *it* was, till suddenly *it* was there and she rose to boiling. The zap of tension that raced up her spine, the shaking of her thighs almost shot Trinity from the bed. Zahid held her hips hard down and his mouth absorbed the energy that pulsed to his lips and tongue as Trinity sobbed out her pleasure. She released a few long-held fears as Zahid fought his—he wanted more, more of the same, more of everything with her. As he lifted her pink and warm from his lips, his mouth suddenly returned again, softly kissing, for he might never be there again.

Trinity wanted to collapse forward but she

was already leaning on her arms as Zahid slid up the bed and let her down so she rested at the top of his thighs.

She looked down where he rose between her legs and just explored him a moment with her fingers. Zahid watched, incredibly turned on by her gentle ministrations, very close to coming for the feel of her on his lips had been incredible and the feel of her hands was sublime.

Trinity stroked what would soon be inside her; she felt the soft drizzle of him moisten her fingers and she was actually excited for the moment ahead. Still breathless from her first orgasm, she wanted to get back on the merry-go-round, loved it that the more she stroked, somehow he became even harder, and bigger too.

'You know…' Trinity said, and then stopped.

'Not unless you tell me.'

'I could get to liking this.' She smiled.

It was the most honest she had been.

'I could get to liking this too,' Zahid said, his face tense from withholding pleasure.

His words were more honest than he should dare to be, for a morning together was becoming far less than enough.

He could not think of that now. His mind was struggling just to remember what had once been routine—he reached to the bedside for a condom. Trinity halted him, for she wanted the softness of his skin to meet hers and she mumbled something about an IUD.

'A coil,' she explained, when he frowned.

She'd had one put in when she'd lost the baby, and had had it changed a couple of years ago, the fear of a random attack almost as petrifying as the fear of getting pregnant again.

'You're sure,' Zahid said, trying to cling onto the last shreds of common sense, for he never went without. 'Because if you get pregnant...' he made a slitting gesture to his throat '...it will be off with mine.' And Trinity actually laughed.

'Very sure.'

He held the base of his thick cock and Trinity lifted herself and lowered herself, loving the feeling of being on top, the control he gave an unwitting gift perhaps, but it set her free.

He filled her completely, she was sure, but then he pulled her hips right down and she shuddered a sob as she struggled to accommodate the full length of him and rose of her own accord to escape, but nature brought her down again. With Zahid her body did not need instruction, it just followed its own lead, until it was Zahid who slowed her down, but for reasons of his own.

He tried to keep things smooth, and although Trinity did her best to move slowly, all she wanted to do was grind against him. Zahid too gave up fighting it and simply let her be.

Was this what she'd been so scared of? Trinity thought as she looked down at Zahid, yet she knew there was no other she could be more herself with. Whatever colour she wore on the day, Zahid saw the person beneath, whatever lie her lips produced, Zahid seemed to extract her truth.

'I think I'm about to come...' Trinity said, and

started to chase the feeling, but to no avail. Just as she thought she might not repeat the magic his mouth had given her, Zahid took over, bucking his hips into her, grinding her down to him, and there was nothing to chase, she was already here. The final swell of him inside and the lift of his hips tipped her over the edge and she came to the delicious sight of a very controlled Zahid momentarily out of it, pulling her down to her side and bucking into her for those last delicious strokes, where they met in a place where logic was left far behind.

It was sex, Zahid said to himself as he kissed her down from her climax. Good-morning sex that had been a long time coming.

It must remain as simple as that.

CHAPTER SIX

IT WAS FAR more complicated, though.

Zahid knew it.

It wasn't just that his people would never accept her as his bride. Or that she might not want to be one.

It went a lot deeper than that.

Zahid rolled away as he did after sex, but then thought twice and rolled back to face her again.

'Penny for them,' Trinity said, and it took a moment for him to register that she was asking his thoughts.

'Oh, it would cost a lot more than that,' Zahid said.

It might cost him his kingdom or, worse, he might lose his head, though not in the way he had joked about before. How could he run a country with Trinity waiting in his bed? How could he focus on his people when his mind would be so consumed by her?

It was no surprise when Trinity turned from his silence and picked up her phone.

Whatever he thought of them, they were her family.

'Eight missed calls,' Trinity said.

'You need to go down?'

'I don't want to,' Trinity admitted, 'but, given that I fly out this afternoon, it would be wrong not to put in an appearance.'

'I know.'

Zahid then made a huge concession. Yes, he had decided to sever ties but for her he would do the right thing. 'Do you want me to come down with you?'

Trinity shook her head and climbed out of bed and started to gather her things.

'What are you doing?' Zahid asked.

'I have to get ready. I need to go to my room.'

'You can get ready here.'

'It's going to be bad enough wearing last night's clothes in the elevator, I'm certainly not going down to face everyone in my brides-maid's dress.'

'Go and have a shower,' Zahid said. 'I will have your things brought here.'

He took care of all the details so easily, Trinity thought as she quickly had a shower and this time she did make a bit of effort with her hair, blasting it with the hotel hairdryer and doing what she could with Zahid's comb.

Now came the hard bit and for once she didn't mean facing her family or facing her fears.

It was facing the man on the other side of the door and pretending what had just happened had been little more than a very pleasant inter-lude.

Now she had to give him up.

Maybe she could go to the pharmacist and ask for Zahid patches, like Donald had when he'd tried to give up smoking, Trinity thought, mak-ing a little joke to herself, trying to lighten the load on her mind. But no gradually reducing dose was going to wean her off Zahid. Trinity knew that already.

Cold turkey, here I come, she decided, opening the door and wearing a smile.

Zahid lay in bed, watching as she put on some make-up and then tied up her hair.

It was over.

He just didn't want it to be.

Or rather he did, for these feelings that he had for her did not sit right with him, these feelings spelt danger.

His mind flicked to his father, bereft on his mother's death, scarcely able to stand, let alone lead a country.

The same would not happen to him.

The dress she had bought for this morning was colourful and floaty and did not quite match her threatening tears as she took the case to the door.

'I'll drop it in my room on the way down.'

Zahid nodded.

So this was goodbye.

'You look beautiful,' he told her, for it was the truth.

'Thank you.'

She ached, not just from him but for him.

'What time is your flight?' Zahid asked.

Trinity told him.

'That is an hour before I am scheduled to fly,' Zahid said.

Their eyes met as they did the maths in their heads, as their brains raced to mental calculators to tap in more time.

One more kiss, one more taste, one more time.

'I could take you to the airport.'

'So I...'

'Leave your case here.'

She almost ran to him. Maybe she did, for suddenly she was back on the bed and in his arms and responding to the fierce promise of his kiss.

'Take as long as you need with your family,' Zahid said as she wrenched herself off, 'but not five minutes more.'

They smiled because they both wanted that little sliver of time before they had to leave.

'Are you sure that you don't want me to join you?' Zahid offered again.

'I'd rather go down on my own.'

She looked at Zahid and there was a moment when she truly wanted to tell him the truth but the very fact that she hadn't meant that, no, he could not join her downstairs.

If he did then it would be a huge disservice to Zahid for, yes, he would do the right thing and make polite small talk with her family, even Clive.

She would not put him, even unwittingly, through that.

'Penny for them,' Zahid said, and Trinity just gave a pensive smile.

'They're not even worth that.'

They weren't, Trinity realised.

Not a pennyworth of thoughts did she want to give to a man who had no place in this room.

'Thank you,' Trinity said, and Zahid's eyes narrowed in a slight frown, for it had been a little joke that she might want to thank him but it sounded like she meant it.

'The pleasure was mine.'

One more kiss, and then just one more, before Trinity headed downstairs to where both Donald's and Yvette's families were gathered. Surprisingly it was a lot easier, knowing that if things got too difficult she could go back up to Zahid.

Even not by her side, he gave her a confidence that she had never had.

'I hear you're working in a library,' Yvette's mother said, and she almost went to correct her but for the sake of peace Trinity lied.

'In the reference section.'

She was the *perfect* daughter, circulating nicely, even pretending that she was listening as her mind roamed several floors upwards. Finally, when she glanced at the clock for the fiftieth time, it was time to say goodbye.

'I'm sorry I got so upset yesterday,' Yvette said as Trinity kissed her goodbye and wished her well for the honeymoon. 'I spoke to Donald last night and it was all just a miscommunication with the hotel.'

'That's good.'

They spoke for a suitable time and Trinity was

just saying her goodbyes to everyone else, silently congratulating herself on a job well done and about to slip away to spend a final, magical hour with Zahid, when Donald pulled her to one side.

'Can I have a word, Trinity?'

She felt her heart sink and just closed her eyes as history repeated itself.

'You know how I hate to ask,' Donald said.

Except it didn't stop him from doing so!

'The hotel is insisting I pay for it all up front. How can I tell Yvette that I've messed up the honeymoon?'

'I haven't got it to give you.' That wasn't the issue, though and, not for the first time, she did her best to face it. 'Donald, you need help.'

'I need my honeymoon,' Donald said. 'It's just been an expensive few weeks. If I can just get away...'

Trinity was too worried to be cross.

So, instead of heading back to Zahid and the bliss of his arms, after a lengthy discussion she sat in the business centre of the hotel and pulled up her account as her time with Zahid slipped ever further away.

She didn't need to ask for Donald's bank details, she had already used them several times.

Thanks to flying economy and saving what she could, Trinity had just over eight thousand dollars in her account. 'How much do you need?'

'Well, there's the hotel, taxis, going out...'

'How much?' Trinity asked, and she couldn't even manage a shrill edge to her voice.

'Whatever you can manage.'

She left herself one hundred dollars and she was too tired from it all to be angry and too scared for her brother to be cross.

'Please, get help, Donald.' She gave him a hug when she stood.

Trinity truly did not know what to do.

She'd begged and pleaded with him over the years, she'd argued and threatened, had offered him the chance to come and stay at hers and just hang out by the beach, but all to no avail. 'I don't want anything to happen to you. I don't want to be at one of these bloody family things without you.'

'I'm fine,' said Donald, peeling her off, only she didn't want to let go.

'I'm scared I'm going to lose you.'

'Honestly, Trinity, there's nothing to worry about.'

'I love you,' Trinity said, 'and so I do worry.'

'Well, there's no need. Thanks for this.'

By the time she'd calmed down and sorted out her make-up to look as if she hadn't been in tears enough to go back to Zahid's room it was already time for she and Zahid to leave for the airport.

'I'm sorry, I got stuck...'

'It's fine.' Zahid pulled her into his arms as their baggage was placed onto a large gold trolley. It wasn't just sex he wanted from Trinity but this, that moment when he held her in his arms and she almost relaxed to him.

He could feel her heart hammering in her chest and, despite a brilliant make-up job, he knew there had been tears, and from the way she clung to him now he doubted that they had been happy ones. 'How was it?'

'Same old, same old,' Trinity attempted, forcing herself to pull back and smile, but she met very serious eyes. 'It was fine,' she said, adding another log to the fire of lies between them.

The traffic was light and in no time they were at Trinity's terminal. Zahid would go onto the VIP section and so they said their final goodbyes in the back of his car. Zahid raised his hand so that no one opened the door to let her out but her luggage was unloaded and it taunted Trinity from the corner of her eye.

'Take me with you.' Trinity smiled. She was joking, sort of, and then she wasn't. There was the threat of tears in her eyes again as she recalled the first time she'd asked him to take her with him. It was combined with this horrible feeling of impending doom.

Zahid had no idea what had happened that terrible night and rather than him see that, she moved in for a kiss, but Zahid halted her, his hand cupping her chin.

'I would love to take you with me,' Zahid said. 'You would be like a breath of fresh air in the palace...' And so very dangerous to his heart. 'You would be the biggest distraction, though.'

Normally, Zahid had no trouble ending things. It was just proving more than a touch difficult now. He actually wanted to take her hand and tell the pilot that there would be another passenger, to take her home to Ishla with him and to hell with consequences.

That was not him, though.

With Trinity he barely recognised himself.

Trinity too was having a lot of trouble remembering that she was supposed to be at ease with this, that it should be easy to simply kiss him goodbye, especially when Zahid started to make promises he surely would not keep.

'Give me your number and I will call...'

'Don't.' She pressed a finger to his lips. 'Don't say you'll call when you won't.'

He stared into very blue eyes and wished he was not going home to start the process of selecting a bride, wished for just a few more months of freedom…but wishes had to be denied when duty called.

'No doubt I'll see you in a few months at a christening.' Trinity attempted a brave smile but it wavered when Zahid shook his head.

Trinity was a luxury that even a married Zahid would find hard to deny.

'I think that this has to be it.'

'Such a terrible shame,' Trinity said, trying to keep things light, trying to pretend this wasn't breaking her heart. 'You could almost make family functions bearable.'

Zahid was struggling too as he tried to relegate it to a one-night stand, or one-morning stand, instead of lovers who were parting for good.

His goodbye was distant.

CHAPTER SEVEN

The cause of death has not been released and the family have requested privacy at this difficult time.

A small, intimate funeral is being held today, followed by a private burial.

THEN THERE WAS the small spiel at the end of the report urging readers struggling with personal issues to 'ring this number'.

No doubt it would be engaged.

Trinity folded the newspaper and put it on the table in front of her as the steward came round.

'Can I get you anything before we start our descent?'

Trinity shook her head and got back to staring out of the window as morning continued to arrive.

She had always feared that this day would

come but only in her worst nightmare had she thought that less than a month after the wedding she would be flying to the same church to say goodbye to her brother for the last time.

It had been a terrible month.

She had mourned Zahid, had ached to call him, to make contact somehow, though knowing that it was not what they had agreed.

No-strings sex, yet her emotions were more than frayed when she'd found out that ten days into their honeymoon Yvette had walked out on Donald and after that her brother had gone spectacularly off the rails.

It had from then on been a rapid descent into hell and Trinity actually couldn't remember when she'd last slept for more than a couple of hours.

Panic had descended when she had first taken the call and heard that Donald had died but it had been quickly replaced by numbness and she was grateful for that as she made her way through customs.

Her mum's family had naturally descended

on the house. Her mother needed her sister but the thought of seeing Clive at this impossible time was more than Trinity could face.

Tonight she would stay at the hotel where the wake was being held before flying back tomorrow.

Yes, another flying visit.

She'd learnt her lesson and so, when her father had transferred money to bring her home for the funeral, she had flown business class this time, but she still hadn't been able to rest.

Heathrow airport saw its share of tears but it didn't glimpse Trinity's today for she held them back, petrified that if one escaped, the floodgates would open.

They nearly did.

As she turned, there was Zahid, the very last person she had been expecting to see, for the funeral was being kept low key. Her mother hadn't mentioned that Zahid would be there when she had spoken to her yesterday.

'You will be okay.'

It was a strange greeting. There was no embrace, just the guidance of his hand on her arm as his driver took her baggage and they were led to his car.

'I wasn't expecting to see you.' Trinity didn't speak till they were in his car. 'Mum said nothing about you coming.'

'I only just found out. By the time I did you had already left for the airport...' Zahid did not elaborate. Now was not the time to tell her that he had finally caved and, unable to get through to Donald, he had rung Dianne to ask for Trinity's number, only to hear the news.

His plane had touched down twenty minutes before hers.

Trinity looked at Zahid. His lips were pale and his features taut. His thick hair was a touch too long and that tiny detail made her frown, for she had never seen him looking anything other than immaculately groomed.

'Let's first get you home.'

'I'm staying at a hotel,' Trinity said. 'You?'

'No hotel—I fly back this afternoon,' Zahid answered. 'When do you go back?'

'Tomorrow.' Her voice was dull and she went back to staring out of the window.

It was not his place to be angered by her lack of duty today. It was not his place to point out that surely she should be by her parents' side, not just for the funeral but in the days that followed.

It did anger him, though, for it just reinforced the fact that she bucked convention, that she refused to do the right thing, especially on a day like today.

They pulled up at the hotel and as the driver removed her luggage Zahid noted the time as they needed to leave soon for the funeral.

'You check in and change. I will wait in Reception.'

'Why?' Trinity said. 'Or are we pretending today that you've never seen me naked before?'

She was, Zahid decided as they headed to her room, the most volatile that he had ever known her and any doubt that he should be here today was erased from his mind.

She needed him today, Zahid told himself,

still fighting that he might need to be with her today too.

'Your mother asked that I deliver the eulogy,' Zahid said, as Trinity tried to plug in her heated rollers then realised that she'd forgotten her adaptor.

'Great!' Trinity hissed, and then turned and gave him a bright smile. 'Great,' she said again.

'In what order?' Zahid asked. 'Is the hiss for the state your hair will be in, or that I have been asked to speak?'

'You choose.'

'Why are you...?' He halted. Now was perhaps not the time to ask why she was so angry at him, now not the time to tell her just the hell this month had been for him too.

'I'm going to have a shower,' Trinity said.

'A quick one,' Zahid warned. 'We have to—'

'I'm not going to be late for my own brother's funeral,' Trinity almost shouted. 'I do know how to tell the time.'

He arched his neck to the side as the bathroom door slammed. Zahid walked on eggshells for no one, yet he could almost feel them crunching beneath his feet as he paced the room.

Leave it for now, he told himself.

Trinity was not his and so he had no right to insist on better behaviour.

She was who she was and in truth he would not change her.

Zahid made a quick phone call and when the adaptor she needed was promptly delivered he sat as she came out from the shower wrapped in a towel and watched her eyes fall on the blinking light of her hair appliance.

Zahid did not expect her to thank him, so her silence came as no surprise.

She flipped open her case and like a depressed magician pulled out black, after black, after black.

Zahid turned his head as she dropped her towel and he heard her snap on her bra, then the sound of her pulling on her panties and then the tear of cellophane as she opened new stockings.

'I'm sorry for the imposition.' Trinity popped

the tense silence with the tip of her anger. 'I know that you never wanted to see me again.'

'Of all your lies, and there are many, that is the biggest.' Zahid looked at her now, appalled at how much weight she had lost this past month, how her skin had paled. He silently berated himself about how much he still wanted her. 'How long did it take you to twist my words into my never wanting to see you again?'

'You said—'

'I said that this had to be it. I said my feelings for you would be inappropriate in the future.' He watched as she started to crumple and he knew enough about Trinity to know that any crumpling would be spectacular and so couldn't happen just yet.

To embrace at the airport would have opened the floodgates but his touch might just hold them closed for a little longer now. 'Come here,' Zahid said, and when she did, he pulled her to his lap.

Her skin did not arouse him this grey morning. Instead, he answered the tiny goose-bumps on her arms and her stomach in their plea for strength and warmth and held her tightly to him. 'I'm here to get you through today,' he said. 'Our stuff can wait. I will call you in a few days and then we can speak properly.' Zahid felt her nod on his chest. 'Today you have enough on your mind without being concerned about us.'

So much on her mind.

Not just that Clive would be there today.

It was the first funeral she had been to since her daughter's, which had been the loneliest day of her life.

'I'm here with you,' Zahid said, and he could never know just how much those words helped. 'Now, get ready.'

He did not avert his eyes as she dressed. There was no point—her scent was on him and his mind would caress her intimately later.

Right now, though, there was a funeral to attend.

As they took their places in the church Zahid recalled their last conversation. *'You could almost make family functions bearable.'*

Nothing could make this bearable, though.

As he stood to read the eulogy, she reminded him of a fragile flower blooming in winter surrounded by the ice of grief.

He looked at Donald's wife, Yvette, whose face was etched in bitterness, and wondered about her pain of the last weeks as her handsome groom had faded to the husband from hell.

Speaking at the funeral of a man you did not admire was a hard task but Zahid executed it well. He spoke of better times, of a younger Donald and family gatherings that...

Zahid glanced up from the notes he had written on the plane. Even as he had penned them he had known that the words were inaccurate, though the right ones to utter, yet Zahid never lied. His eyes turned to Trinity, who started down at black-stockinged knees, and there was the reason he had kept going back. Having admitted that to himself, he was able to speak the truth then. 'Family gatherings that I always looked forward to and will remember with deep affection...' He gave a pale smile as Trinity looked up. 'While we remember the good times,' Zahid said, and looked to Trinity, 'we should not ignore the pain left to us now.'

It was the only time Donald's life was painted as anything other than perfect, Zahid realised as the Fosters micro-managed their son's funeral.

The cemetery was awful. Zahid watched as Trinity held back despite her mother urging her to step forward.

Zahid moved and stood beside Trinity.

The light refreshments were downed with whisky back at the swanky hotel, yet when he wanted to be by her side, the Fosters still kept pulling him away, dragging him into other conversations when he so badly needed to be with her.

He saw her glance at the clock, knew that again they were running out of time and Zahid excused himself from second cousins and made his way over to the one who came first to him. 'How are you?'

'Fabulous!' Her smile was as dangerous as her eyes.

'How are you?' Zahid said again.

'I'm going to lose it in about thirty seconds from now.'

'You're not.'

'I might.'

'You won't,' Zahid said.

Zahid watched as she pushed on a smile as someone approached and offered their condolences but soon it was just them and she told him a little of what was on her mind.

'I don't understand how everyone keeps saying he was a wonderful man, how tragic it was and how sudden. I've been saying for months that this would happen.' She could not stand to be here even a moment longer.

'When do you fly?' Trinity asked.

'In a couple of hours.'

'We could go to my room.'

'I think that would be completely inappropriate,' Zahid said.

'Aww…' Trinity smiled that dangerous smile. 'A playboy with a conscience, how sweet!'

Crunch went the eggshells beneath his well-shod feet. 'You know, Trinity, if it wasn't your brother's funeral…' He halted, not just because Dianne had come over but because of the strength of the words he had been about to deliver, because privately he would like to take her aside and rattle her till she behaved, or tip her over his knee and spank her till she conformed.

He was angry, not just at Trinity but at himself for the foolish moment when he had even considered she might belong by his side, for she could barely behave at her own brother's funeral.

'We've decided to have people back to the house after all,' Dianne informed her daughter.

'I thought the whole point of having it at the hotel was that you wouldn't have to ask people to the house.'

'Well, your father thinks we should ask people back so I need you to go and open up and set up the drinks and glasses—'

'I'm not going back to the house.'

'Trinity…' Dianne had this black smile on in an attempt to disguise the venom in her voice. 'Go and open up and you are to greet—'

'I told you earlier,' Trinity said, 'I'd come to the hotel but I am not—'

'Grow up!' Dianne hissed. 'Grow up and show some respect for your brother's memory.' She walked off and left Trinity standing, her cheeks on fire with years of suppressed rage.

'I will take you back to the house,' Zahid said. He knew today must be agony for her, but there was a part of him that was very cross with Trinity. There were things you did, things that simply had to be done.

He took her rigid hand and led her out to his driver.

'In a couple of hours it will all be over.'

'It will never be over.'

He could not abide her melodrama. Zahid

loathed raw emotion unless it came with an or-gasm attached.

They pulled up at her house and he noticed her cheeks were no longer pink but instead as white as the lilies that had filled the church.

'Let's just set up then I'm going,' Trinity said. She let them in and started to pull out glasses from the dresser as Zahid sorted out the drinks.

Perhaps realising the reception she might get from Trinity, Dianne chose not to ring her daughter when plans changed yet again. Instead, she dialled Zahid. 'Could you ask Trinity to set up the guest room?'

Trinity said nothing at first when Zahid relayed the message, she just marched angrily up the stairs and started pulling towels out of the airing cupboard. 'She's got a bloody nerve.'

Zahid was fast losing his patience. Yes, the Fosters were hard work but Trinity was behaving like a spoilt brat and, frankly, he expected more from her.

'Can you just, for five minutes in your life, do

the right thing?' he said, as Trinity opened the guest-room door. 'Your mother has lost her son.'

She could hear the front door opening and cars pulling up and everyone starting to arrive, and she was past staying quiet, could not hold it in for even a second longer as she stood in the room where so much had been taken from her.

'She's lost more than her son,' Trinity said. 'How dare she pretend that it never happened? How dare she tell me to set up the guest room when she knows full well what went on in here that night?'

'What night?'

'The night *you left me* here!'

Oh, it had been but the tip of her anger back at the hotel, Zahid realised. He knew, with sick dread, the night she was referring to, he knew from the bleached whiteness of her lips and the anguish in her eyes what must have taken place.

He remembered Dianne telling her to set up the guest room for Elaine and Clive and her fingers grasping his as he'd climbed in the car.

Zahid even remembered the time.

Ten minutes after eleven was the moment that now he would regret for ever.

'My aunt's husband...' Trinity gagged. 'After you'd gone, he attacked me.'

CHAPTER EIGHT

ZAHID KNEW THAT how he reacted to this was important to Trinity so he fought for calm as he processed the news, but there was a dangerous instinct kicking in. One that might see him head downstairs this very moment, as the funeral party had now arrived, and for once it would not be their daughter who misbehaved.

'You need to let your parents know,' Zahid said, relieved when he heard his own voice, for it sounded calm, in control, when he felt anything but. 'They need to know what went on that night and why family functions are so hard for you.'

He had always been proud of his self-control but he was in awe of it when she responded to him.

'They know.'

Just two words but they were almost more

than he could process. Zahid could hear long breaths coming out of his nostrils as Dianne called up the stairs for Trinity and he struggled to stay calm. 'Oh, Zahid, your driver said you need to leave.'

'You need to get your flight,' Trinity said, feeling guilty and panicked for telling him and seeing him fight for control. 'Please, Zahid, you can't say anything. It's my brother's funeral.'

He didn't care what day it was.

'Please, don't make this worse for me.'

He pulled her away from the room and wrapped his arms around her in the hall as Zahid for once struggled with what to do.

There were so many reasons not to do what he was about to, so very many, but he simply could not leave her here.

'Usually now you ask to come with me.'

'You always say no.'

'Not this time.' He neither knew nor cared what the reaction would be in Ishla, he just shoved away the thought that in a few days he was to dine with Princess Sameena and her family, then Sheikha Kumu three days after that.

He simply could not leave Trinity here and neither could he stay, because it would be impossible for him not to make a scene.

If his gaze fell on Clive, Zahid knew, there was no telling what he might do.

'You will leave with me.'

'I can't just walk out now.' Even if she had been threatening to just a few minutes ago, the reality was she could not simply walk out and leave, but Zahid had decided otherwise.

'Yes, you can,' Zahid said. 'I will sort it all out. You are not staying here to deal with this alone.' He took her hand and they walked down the stairs and headed to where her parents stood.

'I know it is not the best timing,' Zahid said, 'but I am taking Trinity back to Ishla with me.'

'Sorry?' Dianne blinked.

'I would like to have given you more notice but my return flight has already been arranged.'

So that his eyes would not drift around the room, Zahid stared down Trinity's father and almost dared him to protest, but no one would argue with Zahid in this mood. He was nothing but polite yet there was such a black energy inside him that in a matter of moments they were heading to the airport, only stopping at the hotel to collect her small suitcase.

'I only packed for today. All my things are back in America...'

'You don't need to bring anything,' Zahid said.

'What about work?'

'We'll sort that,' Zahid said, as they neared the airport. 'Tell me where you work and I will call someone.'

'The Beach Bar.' Trinity shook her head. 'It doesn't matter, I'm only casual.'

'I thought...' Zahid halted and let out a breath. He'd spent weeks making phone calls and trying to find out what library it was that she worked out.

Another lie.

What did he know about her?

Even as they boarded his jet, Zahid was quite sure that any minute she would change her mind.

'What will your father say?' Trinity asked.

'Don't worry about that now,' Zahid said. Usually he would let the palace know if he was bringing a guest but in this instance Zahid felt it would be better to speak face to face with his father.

As the plane took to the sky the practicalities of whisking her away were starting to make themselves known. Zahid did think of stopping somewhere en route but there was much for him to do back in Ishla.

He just wanted her away and safe.

She sat beside him and as the plane levelled out in the sky still she said nothing.

'Do you want something to eat or drink?' Zahid asked.

'No.'

'Do you want to rest?'

'No,' Trinity said, but she stood and Zahid watched as she walked towards the sleeping area. Her top was already off. 'I want you to make today bearable.'

'Trinity.' He walked in and watched as she

stripped off her black clothes. 'What you need to understand is that once in Ishla we cannot—'

'What I *need* is one pleasant thing to focus on.'

'Sex won't make this better.'

'Oh, I think you could be wrong.'

'I'm not wrong,' Zahid said. 'When did you last sleep?'

Trinity couldn't answer that. Even thinking up an answer to the most simple question hurt too much right now.

Zahid pulled back the bedding. 'In.'

'I'm naked, Zahid.'

'If that's a problem for you I can see if the stewardess can find something for you to wear to bed.'

'It isn't a problem for me!' Trinity was so cross that he would not be goaded.

'Well, it's no problem for me either. Get some rest,' Zahid said, closing the door on her and taking a seat. But two minutes later she was out, thankfully wearing a robe and blinking at the bright lights.

'Can I have a drink?'

'Do I look like a flight stewardess?' Zahid said, deliberately turning away. 'Press the bell by the bed.'

'I don't want to press the bell.'

He did not turn round and finally she gave in and went back to bed. He watched as a few moments later the stewardess came and answered her call and returned a few moments later with a tray and a glass of sparkling water.

But trying to keep her in bed was like trying to squeeze a jack-in-the-box back into a box with a broken clasp.

'There's a noise.'

She was back again.

'A rattling noise.'

'Possibly because we are on a plane,' Zahid answered. 'Go to bed.'

'I can't sleep,' Trinity said, but she did as told.

For four minutes and forty-five seconds.

'Shouldn't there be a belt—?'

'I'll give you a belt,' Zahid said, standing, and

he practically hauled her into the bedroom and threw her onto the bed.

'A leather one?' Trinity smiled.

'A human one.' He climbed onto the bed but not in it and lay beside her with his arm clamped over her. He turned her round so she was facing away from him but wedged against him.

'Go to sleep,' Zahid said.

'I can't,' Trinity said, 'because if I close my eyes...' So violent was the shudder that racked her, for a moment Zahid wondered if they had hit turbulence, and so loud were the sobs and tears that came then that the stewardess really had no choice but to knock and pop her head into the dark sanctuary in the sky to check if everything was okay.

'She's fine,' Zahid said as the door opened. And the stewardess nodded and closed it as Trinity wailed.

'I don't have tissue.'

'You have a giant one,' Zahid said, placing the sheet in her hand. And not once, as she sobbed, did he tell her to stop or that she should calm down. He just held her facing away from him, clamped down by him, so there was nowhere to hide.

'I gave him money,' Trinity sobbed. 'If I hadn't...'

'I gave him money too,' Zahid said. 'He called me from his honeymoon and said he could not pay the bill. If you want to blame someone, blame me.'

He could take it.

'I paid for his honeymoon,' Trinity said. 'I've lived on noodles for a month.'

'I paid for his honeymoon too, half the wedding party probably paid for his honeymoon,' Zahid said, and his words honed perspective.

He let her cry and then he let her sleep and he should have left then, Zahid knew. He should have climbed from the bed rather than hold her.

Zahid had not slept much in recent weeks either.

With Trinity resting beside him he finally did sleep but a few hours later the first stirring from her had him awake.

'I'm cold,' she moaned to a universe that did not answer.

He pulled the blanket higher on her shoulder then moved her tighter in to his embrace.

'Sleep,' Zahid said. They were five hours into their flight and it was already the most sleep that either had had in a while.

'I'm awake now,' Trinity said. 'Sort of,' she half explained, for she was in that lovely in-between place where things didn't hurt so much, or was it just that Zahid was beside her?

Zahid was beside her and they were on their way to Ishla!

She struggled to duck back into slumber, to not face the problems that surely awaited. He was still on top of the covers and, from the shirtsleeved arm that was over her, still dressed.

And again she was down to her bra and panties and had been put to bed by Zahid.

'Did I demand sex?'

'You did,' Zahid said, and smiled to the back of her hair. Then he remembered the reason she was there and the terrible thing that had happened to her. 'Trinity…'

'I don't want to talk about it.' She had heard the shift in his voice. 'Please.'

'Okay.' That she had told him was huge, Zahid knew.

'Is it going to cause trouble, you bringing me back to Ishla?' Trinity asked.

'Not for you,' Zahid said. 'But...' the ramifications of bringing her home at such a delicate time were starting to hit him. 'It is my birthday in a couple of days...'

'Will there be a party?' she nudged.

'No.' Zahid smiled. 'After that there are dinners to help make the wisest choice when I choose my bride.'

'Choose me,' Trinity said, and put her hand up in the air as if answering a question in class, and they both laughed. 'I've never heard you laugh,' Trinity said, as his hand came up to join hers.

'Neither have I,' Zahid said, capturing her raised hand and holding it there.

'Will you serve me without question?' Zahid said.

'I won't.'

He felt the resistance as she tried to pull her arm down and it was a game but a sad one for possibly the only way they could discuss it was to have a little play. 'Do you promise to remember to do your duty as I serve my country.'

'I don't.'

'And I don't need to ask if you will obey...' He released her hand and she moved it down and turned to face him and stared unblinkingly into his eyes.

'The closer you get,' Trinity said, 'the kinder you look.'

'The closer you get, the less I can see.'

'Can I be your mistress?'

'I would never take a mistress,' Zahid said. 'Which is why I would not have been at any christening.' She worried him so. 'Why would you want to be a mistress?'

'It was a joke, Zahid.' Trinity tried to turn it into that. In fact, she didn't want to be a mistress, just something of his.

'So how will you decide who will be your bride?'

'Alliances.'

She turned onto her back and chose to stare at the ceiling for she did not like his detached answer and it did not sound like him, or rather it did not sound like the Zahid that only she saw. 'So you'll marry for alliances with the hope love will grow?'

'Love is for fools and peasants, not for a future king.'

'Thanks,' Trinity said, and she turned and watched his haughty face twitch into a slight smile. 'Then I'm either a fool or a peasant.'

'I was not talking about you.'

'Of course you are. Just because you are going to be king one day, you think feelings are beneath you…'

'I am telling you how it is in my land,' Zahid said, refusing to be swayed. 'I am telling you my reasoning.' But not all of it. He chose not to tell her about his father's illness and when Layla had been born, for he could not share that with another and remain aloof, could not return to that memory and somehow stay detached, yet he knew to be fair to Trinity he must make things clear. 'I am telling you that in Ishla things will be very different between us.' He went to get up. 'I will have some refreshments brought in to you and then you should get dressed as we need to be out there when the plane starts its descent.'

'I know things will be different but we're not in Ishla yet,' Trinity said, as he rose from the bed and went to the door and she waited, breath held as Zahid halted and went against his own moral code, just for that one last time with her.

She watched as he turned and then undressed and it was Trinity who held the covers open this time. Naked beside him, it felt as if she had been cold for the entire month and had just remembered how it felt to be warm. 'Thank you,' Trinity said.

'I haven't done anything yet.'

'For making me happy. I shouldn't be happy today but I am.'

'You should be happy every day,' Zahid said,

for even on the worst days they made the other smile.

His mouth was tender. It was a slow and long kiss for even if they did not have very long he still did not rush her.

Slow was the hand that explored her, that stroked her breasts and then her hips, and Trinity could feel the building need in him. When she rolled to her back, when he moved deep into her, Zahid took his own weight on his elbows and their kissing stopped and he looked down at Trinity as she looked back at him.

She felt him build, yet she felt him hold back and it was his passion she wanted.

'You don't have to be careful around me.'

She saw the twist of pain on his lips, for the news had devastated him, she knew.

'You don't have to hold back,' Trinity said, because she wanted the Zahid who wanted her as she was, with no thought what had been. And right now she wanted his anger, for she was angry too and had every right to be—this was their last time. 'Please don't hold back on me, Zahid.'

He took her the way he wanted to and drove hard into her, but far from scaring her he drove her fear away, for her hands were pressing him in and her body was arching to his as they both refused to allow anything other than themselves in the bedroom.

It was Zahid who shouted and to feel him unleash just unravelled her more.

Deep, intense, blissful was the orgasm that met his and Trinity did her best not to cry out, but did and then frantically glanced at the door, but he brought her face back with his hand and his mouth took her moans and there was nothing she was scared of with Zahid.

'You were right,' Zahid said, looking down at the woman he would crave for ever. 'My feelings are beneath me.'

It took a moment for Trinity to understand his words.

Yes, his feelings lay beneath him right now, every one of them contained in her.

As a bell warned that they would soon be descending, Zahid knew he must leave feelings here.

He just wasn't sure how.

They quickly washed and dressed but instead of putting on his suit, for the first time she saw him in robes and wearing a *kafiya*.

He saw her startle.

'I...' She didn't know what to say. 'It all seems a bit more real now.'

'I don't know if I am making things worse for you,' Zahid admitted, for it had simply seemed right to bring her when he had found out what had happened. The reality, though, made little sense.

'I don't want to meet the women you'll...'

'I know.'

For the first time jealousy stirred in Trinity and despite herself she wanted to know more.

'Must she be a virgin?'

'Trinity, we need to get back to our seats,' Zahid said, for he did not want to discuss his future wife now.

'So you're not going to answer my question?'

'She must have kept herself only for me.'

He went to open the door but her words halted him. His kiss, his lovemaking, the way he had been with her had changed her world and Zahid deserved to know the gift he had given to her. 'I have.'

She saw the line between his eyes deepen as he tried to fathom her words.

'There's been no one but you, apart from...'

'Don't,' Zahid said. 'Don't put the two together, for what that bastard did does not count in any land that I would rule.' He did not know what to believe. 'Trinity, the woman I took to bed that day was confident...'

'Not at first,' she admitted. 'Zahid, I've had issues since that night, I've tried so many things. I know I flirt, I know I seem bold but that's how I am with you...'

'I should have known!' Zahid said. 'I would have done things differently.'

'Exactly!' Trinity said, as the bell carried on pinging and then there was a knock on the door.

Zahid called out something in Arabic.

'Had I told you the truth, would it have happened?' When Zahid didn't answer, Trinity did for him. 'Of course not.'

'You *should* have told me.'

'No.' Trinity shook her head. 'Because then it would never have happened and I refuse to regret that it did. I know it can't happen again,' she said. 'I get it that it doesn't change things.'

But for Zahid it did.

CHAPTER NINE

TRINITY HAD NEVER really given his land much thought but as they neared she looked down at and knew it was not what she might have expected.

Old married new, for there were ancient villages, yet as they flew along the peninsula she saw too the high glitter of modern architecture, but most beautiful by far was the palace for it gleamed the brightest all.

'It's amazing.' When she got no response she glanced over at Zahid, whose face might have been carved from one of the stone palace walls.

'Zahid....'

There was no chance to talk. The plane was a second from landing and as it hit the palace runway, Zahid was actually grateful for the jolt of landing and the sound of wheels on the tarmac for it gave him two seconds away from his thoughts.

He had been her first.

He needed to process it, they needed to discuss it, but first somehow he had to clear his head.

A car drove them the short distance from the plane and though Zahid's driver did his best to keep his face impassive, Trinity could feel him repeatedly glancing in the rear-view mirror. It was the same when they arrived. The maids gaped in surprise as Prince Zahid arrived with a blonde foreigner dressed only in black and Trinity stood, her face burning, as Zahid spoke to a man in Arabic, who then walked off.

'That is Abdul, my father's chief aide, I have told him to let my father know that I wish to speak with him and to have a suite arranged for you.' He halted and turned as a very beautiful, raven-haired woman walked towards them with a curious expression on her face. 'This is my sister, Layla.'

'And this is?' Layla asked, when for once Zahid forgot his manners.

'Trinity,' Zahid responded, and Trinity watched as Layla raised an eyebrow and waited for her brother to elaborate. 'Trinity Foster.'

'It is lovely to meet you, Trinity,' Layla said.

'I am about to let Father know that I have a guest,' Zahid said. 'Layla, perhaps you could help Trinity to settle in and sort out some clothes and things for her. She came at short notice and so has nothing much with her.'

'Of course.' Layla smiled. 'This way.'

They were all so terribly polite, Trinity thought. Surely Layla must have a thousand questions but instead a maid was called and they drank mint tea as they waited for her room to be readied.

The king, though, did not hold back.

'Zahid,' the king said sharply. 'You said you wanted nothing more to do with that family...'

'I was not referring to Trinity when I said that.' He looked at his father.

'Perhaps,' the king said, 'but here the rules are different.'

'I am aware of that.'

'Here, you are not the man you are overseas.'

'I have brought Trinity here as a friend as, not for anything else.'

'It is not respectful to your future bride to be housing your mistress!'

'She is not my mistress,' Zahid said, for she no longer was. They had said their intimate good-byes on the plane.

'Then why is she here?'

'For pause,' Zahid said. 'She has just lost her brother and there are family issues.'

'What does that have to do with you?'

When Zahid did not respond the king breathed out loudly. 'You are to say to Abdul that she is here to help Layla with her English.'

'Why lie?'

'It is not a lie,' Fahid said. 'Layla is, after all, helping to teach the girls of Ishla English and, given you have many functions and dinners to attend in the coming days, I assume it will be Layla who entertains her.'

'Yes.'

'And that will help Layla's English.'

'Fine,' Zahid said, and he looked at his father and saw he was visibly worried, for Zahid had never brought any friends from England, let alone a woman, back to the palace. 'It is just for a few days. You will hardly see her...'

'Why would I not greet your guest? Why, if you have nothing to hide, is she to be tucked away?' The king would prefer to confront the enemy, the woman who could seemingly so easily sway his son from the marriage that the king had in mind for Zahid. 'Tonight we will dine, and I would like to meet your guest'

'Trinity is tired from her travels.'

'Then we will dine early. Layla has to teach in the morning anyway.'

'It is nothing to be nervous about,' Layla said after Zahid had told Trinity a little later that she would be dining with the king tonight. 'You won't be expected to say much.'

Trinity smiled at Layla's rather wry comment.

'I talk too much,' Layla said, 'I question things and it itches my father.'

'Irritates,' Trinity corrected her, and Layla frowned. 'It irritates your father.' Trinity explained but she watched as Layla's cheeks turned pink. 'Zahid just said I was to help you with your English.'

'My English is perfect,' Layla said. 'Don't correct me again.'

Whoa!

They were all terribly polite, Trinity amended, *if* you remembered your place.

Yet Layla, in her own, very odd way, was lovely. 'Try this.' She held up a lilac tunic for Trinity but as soon as she tried it on, both women realised it was far too tight. It clung instead of hung and gave her more curves than were polite in Ishla.

'Oh, no.' Layla laughed, making the same cut throat gesture that Zahid once had. 'Try this one instead.' But as she handed her a pale mint one that would hopefully fit better, Trinity suddenly stopped smiling as she stared at her refelction.

Yes, she had lost a lot of weight this past month, just not from her breasts—for once she actually filled her bra.

Layla misread the sudden silence.

'I am sorry you lost your brother. I would die if something happened to Zahid.'

'We weren't very close in the last few years,' Trinity admitted.

'It must hurt.'

'It does,' Trinity said, 'but I am very angry with him at the moment.'

It felt strange to be able to speak with Layla, who she had only just met, more easily than she could with her parents.

'There are other hurts,' Trinity said, glad when Layla did not ask her to elaborate.

Only it wasn't the other hurts that were worrying Trinity now.

As she slipped the tunic over her head, that brief second of privacy had Trinity's face screw up in a frantic, silent panic as she willed her brain to remember her last period, but with all that had happened since that day, the last month was a painful blur.

'That's better.' Layla smiled and helped Trinity arrange the tunic. 'There are some lovely gold slippers that go nicely with it, or these jewelled ones, which I think would go really well.'

'The gold are beautiful…'

'But I prefer the jewelled ones,' Layla said.

She was in Ishla, Trinity reminded herself as she accepted Layla's suggestion, but even a detail like slippers served to remind Trinity that she knew nothing about this strange land.

Zahid was rather nervous both for Trinity and himself.

He watched as she walked in and after a flurry of introductions took a seat on a low cushion. He was grateful to Layla, who quickly moved Trinity's feet so her soles were facing away from the king.

'My son tells me you live in America?'

'I have for a few years.'

'You studied?'

'Ancient art history.'

'You must take Trinity to the second palace.' The king looked at his son. 'I am sure she would be interested. Perhaps Trinity would like to start the cataloguing.'

'Trinity is not here to work.'

'It wouldn't be work.' Trinity smiled. 'I didn't know there was a second palace. I don't remember seeing it as we came in to land.'

'It is hidden,' the king said. 'I am sure Zahid will be grateful for that in the coming year.'

'Coming year?'

'Once married, Zahid will live there with his bride until it is time for him to be king.'

Trinity reached for her water. Suddenly the thought of going there, seeing first hand where Zahid would live, held little appeal, but taking a cool drink she forced her smile brighter and Zahid could only admire her composure, for he knew his father was goading her for a reaction.

'And then Zahid will rule from here,' the king continued.

'Well, you'll need a lot of baby gates.' Trinity smiled sweetly, looking around at the many treasures.

'The future princes and princesses shall not live here till they come of age.' The king's explanation only added to her confusion. 'There are many treasures at the second palace too but, you are right, it is less formal. A lot of the artefacts at the second palace have significant, personal meaning.'

There were treasures everywhere. Even the plate she was picking up sticky rice from could have held her attention for an hour or more. Gold and blue, the more she ate, the more of the pattern it revealed, and Trinity would have loved to simply clear it and turn it around.

'You should take Trinity over there tomorrow,' the king said to Layla.

'I have a class to teach tomorrow,' Layla said.

'And I would be the worst person to attempt to catalogue a palace.' Trinity smiled. 'It would never get done.' She looked at the plate again and then at the king. 'Among so many beautiful things, do you have favourites?'

Zahid caught Layla's eye, both waiting for the king to silence her, yet the king actually forgot to be cross for a moment and smiled. 'I do, though I have not looked at them in a long time. My wife collected amulets, they are stored in a mandoos, or rather, a wooden chest.'

'In the second palace?'

'No,' the king said. 'I had it moved here, not that I have looked through it in a while.'

They spoke easily through dinner but then the king turned to Layla.

'Perhaps it is time for you to retire,' the king said to his daughter, 'if you want to be alert for your students tomorrow.'

Zahid caught Trinity's eye for a brief second and again they were back in the woods, Zahid reminding her how much freedom she had, for he could not imagine Trinity at seventeen, let alone Layla's twenty-four, being told, however politely, to go to bed.

After dinner they drank coffee that would surely keep Trinity awake till the small hours but soon the king retired, leaving Zahid to walk Trinity back to her quarters.

'You did well,' Zahid said.

'I wasn't aware it was a test,' Trinity snapped.

'I was just commenting...' Zahid halted. 'You are tired, it has been a long day. Perhaps...'

'Please, don't try to tell me when I need to go to bed again.'

'I wasn't,' Zahid said. 'I was going to suggest we take a walk on the beach. I thought that might relax you.'

'Isn't it forbidden?'

Zahid said nothing and they walked through the moonlit night, past the palace, but as Trinity turned in the direction of what she assumed was the path to the beach, Zahid's hand gripped her arm and halted her.

'It is this way.'

'Oh,' Trinity said, 'so where does that lead?' She saw his face shutter, acknowledged his lack of response to her question and, realising it was the entrance to the second palace, she let out a mirthless laugh.

'Trinity, I am sorry if my father upset you tonight but I have never lied, I have never tried to hide my truth.' His eyes were accusing. 'Unlike you.'

'I've told you why I couldn't tell you.'

'Have you?' Zahid said. 'You tell me only the pieces you want me to know and at a time of your choosing.'

'That's not true.'

'Are you sure?' Zahid asked, for she had lied about her workplace, her sexual history and he knew she had been in rehab too. 'Are you sure you are as honest with me as I am with you?'

Trinity tugged her arm away. She wanted to talk to him, to speak with Zahid, to tell the only person on this earth she could, just how deep her pain went, but for what? At a time of Zahid or the king's choosing she'd be gone. She was scared too to tell him that she was starting to worry about her absent period. She doubted either of them would go unnoticed if they bought a pregnancy test!

'What am I doing here, Zahid?' It was like waking up from a dream. This morning she had been at her brother's funeral, this afternoon she had found herself safe in his arms, and now she was walking deep in the night on a beach in Ishla. Trinity honestly didn't know what part of the day had hurt the most—losing her brother, losing her heart or losing to this strange land. 'Why did you bring me here?'

'Because, given what you told me, I could not leave you with them.'

'I can't hide here for ever.'

'I'm not asking you to hide.'

The beach was as white as powder and the sea the colour of her bridesmaid's dress but with more depth, and Trinity battled the urge to run along the beach and leave footprints or write their names in the sand and watch the ocean take them away.

'It's like paradise,' Trinity sighed, 'but with separate bedrooms.'

They faced each other and it was simply wrong not to be in the other's arms.

'What do you want?' Zahid asked.

'To wake up and not fancy you any more,' Trinity said. 'For even the sound of your voice to annoy me.'

'I hope for the same,' Zahid said. They both smiled reluctantly. 'Nag me.' He smiled again.

'Take up fishing and talk to me endlessly about it.'

They both wanted a kiss, even a touch would do, but it could not happen here.

Ever.

CHAPTER TEN

TRINITY WAS THE perfect guest.

Well, not perfect, for the palace was a little less ordered when she was around.

Zahid woke on the morning of his birthday to a folded piece of paper under his door and he was at first cross when he opened the makeshift card from Trinity, for she should not be wandering at night near his room.

Her words wished him a happy birthday but there was the notable absence of kisses under her name, just a smiley face and two words.

Better not!

And there was a stick figure, Zahid with a fishing rod.

He was no longer cross.

Once he was dressed in full military regalia, Zahid glanced to his bedside where the paper card lay.

Zahid did not keep mementos and he did not know what to do with this, for if he left it in his room, the maids would no doubt think it rubbish. If he put it in his drawer, perhaps it became more than it was.

A memento.

He pulled on long leather boots with a head that was pounding, for even dressed as heir to the throne, even about to greet his people, Zahid's mind was full of her.

He would decide what to do with the makeshift card later, Zahid decided, folding it and putting it in his pocket for now.

As he walked briskly to his father's study he met Trinity on the way.

'Happy birthday, Captain.' She smiled and though they stood a suitable distance apart as she teased him lightly about his uniform they were back on the dance floor and the dirty dance started again, when it must not.

'Thank you for the card,' Zahid said, 'but it was unwise to come up to my room.'

'Oh, well.' Trinity shrugged.

Zahid gave her a small nod and then walked off but his stride was temporarily broken when she wolf-whistled.

Possibly he blushed.

Possibly not, Zahid quickly decided. Most likely he was cross.

'Where is Layla?' Zahid asked, as he joined his father in his study.

'She is late again,' came the king's curt response.

They did not do 'happy birthdays'.

Layla was happily late. Besotted with Trinity and when she should be meeting with her father and brother, she smiled widely when Trinity knocked and Jamila, Layla's handmaiden let Trinity into her room.

'I got a message that you wanted to speak with me,' Trinity said.

'I want you to join me when I take one of my English classes.'

'I'd be happy to.' Trinity smiled.

'Tomorrow,' Layla said, Jamila finished doing her hair and make-up.

'That would be lovely,' Trinity said, for to-morrow Zahid dined with Princess Sameena and her family and it would be nice to have her mind on other things.

'Walk with me,' Layla said, and Trinity suppressed a smile, for she could not be offended by the way Layla ordered people around, she was completely used to getting anything she asked for. 'We can talk on the way.'

Layla told her about the students she taught and how much she enjoyed the contact, even if it was online. 'It is by video call,' she explained, 'which means I can get to most of the schools. We have a lot of fun and they will be so excited to meet a real English girl.'

'I'm excited to meet them too.'

'They ask so many questions,' Layla sighed. 'Difficult ones.'

'Such as?'

'You'll see,' Layla said. 'I had better hurry. I am already terribly late and my father will be cross that I am not already there.'

He was, especially when a maid informed him that Layla was chatting with Trinity.

'Just how long is your guest here for?' Abdul checked as they went through the briefing for in a few moments they would walk onto the balcony.

'I am not sure,' Zahid said, ignoring Abdul's slight eye rise, but the king spoke on.

'Today there is much celebration in Ishla. Not only does the future king celebrate his birthday but work is to commence on the second palace.' He looked at his son. 'Soon the people will find out who their prince is to marry.'

This time it was Zahid who asked Abdul if he could excuse them.

'I would like the dinners to be postponed,' Zahid said.

'It is far too late for that. Princess Sameena and her family are joining us tomorrow,' the king said. 'And why would you want them postponed?' He dared his son with his eyes to answer him.

Zahid accepted the dare.

'I would like to spend more time with Trinity.'

'Before you make a commitment to marry a suitable bride?' the king checked, and when Zahid did not answer he continued speaking. 'Because you know that Trinity Foster would be a most unsuitable bride and one that the people would never accept.'

'My answer to your question was the correct one. I would like to spend more time with Trinity.' That was all Zahid wanted. Time for Trinity to get used to Ishla and perhaps see its beauty. Time in England as a couple to see if they could work things out.

Time even to find out that they were not suited for each other, Zahid thought, recalling their conversation last night and the card in his pocket with the stick-figure picture on. He did his best not to smile.

Yes, all he wanted was time, and he looked at his father. 'You know I have never made a decision lightly.'

'You understand the offence that would be caused if these dinners were postponed.'

Zahid swallowed, for he did not want to make problems for his country. 'I do.'

'And you know that I want a wedding, so if I postpone these dinners then I shall invite the Fayeds for dinner next Sunday?'

'Father.' Zahid was not interrupting the king for his own benefit. Layla had just walked in unseen by the king and her eyes widened in horror as she heard what was being discussed. 'Hassain too,' the king continued. 'I would like to speak first hand with the man who will soon marry my daughter.'

'No!' Layla screamed, and the king turned as she ran from the room.

'Layla,' Zahid roared as he went to chase his sister, but she had flown straight into a shocked Trinity's arms.

'What's happening?'

'Layla is overreacting,' Zahid said. 'Layla, what you heard was the end of a very difficult conversation…' But Layla would not be consoled. 'You need to calm down so we can go out to the balcony, and then I will explain properly.'

'I'm not going out there,' Layla sobbed.

Abdul approached and told them that the king was making his way to the balcony and it was time for Zahid and Layla to join him.

'No!' Layla wept. 'You can't make me.'

'Layla.' Zahid was stern, for he was used to dealing with his sister's dramas and all too often it fell to him to calm her down, but the reproach in his voice made Trinity shiver. 'First you will do what is right *then* we will talk.'

He ignored Trinity's raised brows and the purse of her lips as Layla joined her brother, but he could not ignore the disquiet of standing, smiling at his people, as his sister stood, not scowling for the camera, as Trinity once had, but meek and fearful for her future, by his side.

'You said I did not have to worry for a while...' Layla said once they were back inside, but her voice trailed off as her father entered the room.

The world, Zahid thought wearily, was far less complicated when it was faced without emotion.

'I need an answer from you, Zahid,' the king warned.

'And I told you I do not make decisions lightly.'

It was an impossibly long day. A formal lunch and then he inspected the army and later a semi-formal dinner that Trinity did attend, but she sat next to a red-eyed Layla. For once it was easy for Trinity to sit quietly, for she had a horrible taste in her mouth. A *familiar,* horrible taste in her mouth, and she took a sip of the fragrant tea at the end of the meal. It tasted like neat perfume.

When would her period come?

After dinner, when Trinity had excused herself to go to her room, Zahid asked to speak with Layla. It was not an easy conversation to have.

'I asked Father if he could postpone the dinners so that I could spend more time with Trinity.'

'You love her?' Layla frowned, for she could not imagine her stern older brother falling in love, as his focus had always been his country.

'You too!' Zahid rolled his eyes. 'I am supposed to give an immediate answer when I am trying to make up my mind what is for the best, not just by my people but by Trinity, by you too...'

'Of course you love her,' Layla challenged, 'or you would not have brought her here and be asking to postpone dinners.'

'Away from here, people date, they get to know each other, they see if their differences will work better together, or if they should be apart...'

'You think I feel sorry for you?' Layla sneered. 'Well, I don't. You are going to be king, of course you must marry a suitable bride, but at least you have known love in your lifetime, at least you got to be free for a while before you started your family.' Layla started to cry. 'So don't ask me to understand how d ifficult things are for you when the man I will marry and spend all my life with is Hassain.'

She ran crying to her room and Zahid walked in the grounds, but it did not relax him because the day replayed over in his head.

He turned and looked as a noise disturbed him. He saw shutters open but he looked away when he realised it was Trinity's suite.

Perhaps she couldn't sleep either, Zahid thought; perhaps the air in her room was as stifling as it was out here, for there was no escape from his thoughts.

His eyes moved back to her window and he could only sigh as he watched her peek out and then turn.

One foot, followed by the other.

Zahid walked over quietly as Trinity shimmied down the short drop from her window.

'Are you averse to using doors?'

When she heard Zahid, Trinity jumped.

'I wanted to go for a walk.'

'So why use the window?'

'I didn't know if I could.'

'It is not a prison.'

'You told me this morning that I should not be wandering the palace at night.'

'I meant you should not be near my room.'

'Oh, please...' Trinity started, then halted, for

last night the temptation had been great to creep in. Not that she would tell him that. 'There are so many rules, I'm never sure if I'm breaking one or not.'

'Just be yourself.'

'You're not, though,' Trinity pointed out. 'I barely recognised you when you told Layla off this morning.'

'Layla was upset. It was the only way to calm her down.'

'Perhaps, but I don't really know you at all, Zahid.' He didn't respond. 'Does anyone?'

'What do you want to know?'

'You. What you think about things, how you feel, or are you going to tell me again that feelings are beneath you?'

'I have not been fair to you,' Zahid said, and stopped walking. 'Perhaps it was easier to blame your past and your ways on the fact that we cannot have a future but it is more complicated than that.'

'It is,' Trinity said, 'because even if I didn't have a past I'm not sure I'd want...' She gave a shrug and Zahid waited but Trinity didn't say any more. Instead, it was Zahid who spoke on and told her a little of his family's history.

'My father was to choose Raina as his bride, a princess from a neighbouring land who is now Queen. The marriage would have profited our people, ensured swift progress. Instead, progress has been painfully slow.'

'Why didn't he choose her?'

'My father walked into the room and saw my mother. She had been crying because she did not want a loveless marriage and to be chosen by the future king, but then their eyes met and she changed her mind. My father says she smiled at him and in that moment his choice was made.'

'Did it cause problems?'

'Many,' Zahid said. 'It caused division and even today relations are strained. That can be rectified now, though, if I choose Raina's daughter, Sameena.'

'Oh, so you do lie, Zahid!' Trinity said. 'You told me that you hadn't chosen.'

'I haven't,' Zahid said. 'I would prefer not to go with the elders' choice because one of the other potential brides comes from a country with a very organised army—'

'I don't want to hear,' Trinity said, for she did not want to hear about any future wife, but she did want to know about the marriage of his parents and all the trouble that it had caused. 'Were your parents happy?'

'Yes, they were happy, while their people bore the cost of a decision made in a rash moment.' Zahid shrugged. 'And then, when my mother died, their king fell apart. That is what love does to a man. When I saw how my father crumbled on my mother's death I decided I wanted no part in a marriage that made one so weak. My father could barely move from his bed. What if there had been trouble with neighbouring countries, what if there had been an emergency and decisions had been needed to be made? He was incapable.'

'I doubt that could ever happen to you.'

'I never thought it would happen to my father,

yet it did,' Zahid said. 'I want no part in a love that renders you incapable.'

It was a very backhanded way of revealing his feelings but Trinity just shrugged and started walking, thinking over his words. They actually made a lot of sense to her.

'So you want your own Dianne?'

'Excuse me?'

'Your own Dianne, standing smiling and plastic by your side and agreeing, without question, to whatever you decide.'

'Do not compare me...' He caught her arm and swung her round. It was rather a difficult conversation because to reveal the absolute insult that was meant that he had to criticise Trinity's parents, but another Dianne was the very last thing he wanted from his wife. 'I do not want that from a wife.'

'You told me so yourself. You want a wife who will obey and serve without question,' Trinity challenged. 'That's what my mother does, she stands idly by.'

'Your father has made many mistakes.'

'Oh, and you're exempt from making them?' Trinity checked. 'I'm sure my father would insist he was only doing the best for his family and constituents, that my mother doesn't understand what it takes to do the job he does. I'm quite sure if he loved her he wouldn't have had those affairs and I'm quite sure he blames her for what happened to me. It was her side of the family after all.'

Zahid stood there a touch breathless, furious at her challenge, reluctantly acknowledging her words.

'I don't want my past pardoned in some grandiose gesture,' Trinity said, 'only to be thrown back at me, and, no, I would never stand with a plastic smile, meekly accepting that you know best.' She gave him a bright smile. 'See, we're completely incompatible, but it works both ways, Zahid. I don't want your idea of a marriage. I want a love that burns and sometimes hurts, one that challenges me at every turn. I want a father for my children who does not hold onto his emotions, whatever the cost.' The ab-

sence of her period had Trinity for once thinking ahead and what she saw was not pretty. 'I
don't want a family tucked away in the second
palace, with their father an occasional guest,
till they come of age and can move to the main
one...'

'You don't understand.'

'I don't, Zahid.' She smiled a plastic smile
that infuriated him. 'But that's okay—clearly, I
don't have to. I just have to agree to your ways.'

'I would always do the right thing by my family but there are rules in place and those rules
mean I must do the right things by my people.'

'Yes, Zahid.'

'And I would never cheat on my wife.'

'Yes, Zahid.'

'Stop agreeing with me.'

'Oh, sorry, I thought that was what you
wanted.' Then she smiled a very slow smile
and his face was rigid as she made him exam-
ine a truth. 'Why did we have to sever contact?'

'You know why.'

'Are you worried that you couldn't keep your hands off me, even with a wife by your side?'

'No!'

'Oh, just those pesky inappropriate thoughts, then.' Trinity winked. 'Well, that's okay, then,' she said, and ran off towards the palace.

Never, not once, had anyone challenged him so; never once had he questioned his own integrity so much; never had he wanted to chase someone so much, to catch her and turn her round, to press her to the jewelled palace wall and demand she retract her words.

And Zahid did just that. In a moment he had caught up with her and, yes, he pushed her to the wall but in the way that lovers did and he demanded then that she take back what she'd said.

That she retract.

'Retract what?' Trinity asked.

The truth.

She looked deep into his eyes, could feel his erection pressed into her, and she just stared and challenged him to kiss her, to break the strange rules of this beautiful land. And then she did the unforgivable. She smiled, the plastic smile of her mother, and Zahid pulled back, staring into the tempting pool of her mouth and trying to shift decades of thinking as his mouth moved towards her, but Trinity turned her head.

'I'm going to bed, Zahid, presumably alone.'

'Stay.'

'No!' Trinity said. 'I'm too good for a shag against the palace wall.'

'I would not do that to you.'

'You want to, though.' Her hand reached down and what met her hand did not deny the truth.

But though she returned alone to her room, Trinity did not go to bed.

She couldn't be pregnant, Trinity thought as she lifted her leg on the bed and pushed her fingers inside, feeling for the strings that would tell her the IUD was in place, but was unable to find them. She felt behind her cervix hoping to find them nestling there but, no, they were nowhere to be found.

Trinity undressed and examined her body. Apart from slightly bigger breasts, there were no changes she could see. She didn't feel sick, she felt exactly as she always had. In fact, better than she always had, for the most part. Here in Ishla she was relaxed.

Not now, though.

She remembered Zahid's slitting gesture to the throat and how she had laughed at the time.

She wasn't laughing now.

CHAPTER ELEVEN

LAYLA WAS NOT quite so gushing with Trinity the next morning.

'Is everything okay?' Trinity checked, as they walked to her study where Layla would take her class.

'If Zahid does not choose his bride, the next bride will be me.'

'That is not what you want?'

Layla's black eyes met Trinity's. 'It would seem that it has nothing to do with what I want.'

'Layla.' Trinity's hand went to her shoulder, but Layla shrugged it off.

'Please, don't,' Layla said. 'I am cross with you even though deep down I know it is not your fault. I will not stay cross for long.'

They were all so honest, Trinity thought, but in the nicest of ways, because where else could you deny a touch because of the mood you were in?

Here they did not pretend.

'Do you want to do the class tomorrow?' Trinity offered.

'No,' Layla said. 'I have promised the girls that you will meet them today, they would be so disappointed if that did not happen. I too have told them that you are here in the palace to help me with my English but you are not to correct me in front of them. It is easier to say that than explain you are here to sabotage my life.' She saw Trinity startle. 'Sorry, was "sabotage" the wrong word?'

'I'm not allowed to correct you,' Trinity pointed out, and Layla narrowed her eyes.

'You can with my permission.'

Trinity thought for a moment. 'Actually sabotage is the perfect word. I'm so sorry, Layla.'

'See! I was right,' Layla said, but then she smiled. 'I know it was unintentional, though,' she said, and gave Trinity a hug.

They were friends again.

English with Princess Layla was far more fun than Trinity remembered her English lessons to be!

Really, it was more an hour of conversation, for Layla did not know how to read or write in English.

Layla did not know how to drive either, Trinity found out as the questions poured in from Layla's students and one of them asked how you would get to school in England if you did not have a driver like Princess Layla.

'You would walk, or get a bus or train,' Trinity said.

'I would take my driver,' Layla said, and they all laughed at the thought of their princess walking, or getting a bus or train, and so too did Layla.

It was fun.

Till the topic turned to weddings.

'Does the bride wear gold in England?' a little girl asked.

'She wears white,' Trinity said, wondering if it might be a touch difficult to explain just how diverse weddings could be. 'Well, traditionally she wears white.'

'We are going to say goodbye to Trinity now,'

Layla broke in swiftly, for she knew they would have many questions about weddings and it was something neither woman would, today, choose to discuss.

They all said goodbye and thanked her but still the questions came for Layla.

'My mother says that our prince is going to marry soon,' the same little girl said. 'Princess Layla, will they live at the second palace?'

'That is private,' Layla warned, which went against everything Layla's classes were about, it was why the students loved her so.

'You said, so long as we asked politely and in English, that you would answer our questions.'

Layla closed her eyes for a brief moment. 'Yes,' Layla said. 'Our tradition says that the future king will live at the second palace with his bride until it is time for him to rule.' She looked at Trinity, who had moved away from the camera and had tears streaming down her face.

It was cruel to hear about Zahid's future life

and Layla nodded when Trinity stood. 'I'm going to go for a walk.'

'Of course.' Layla nodded. 'Wait one moment,' she said to her students, 'and I will be back.' She joined Trinity at the door. 'I am so sorry.'

'It's not your fault. Of course they have questions.'

'You did not need to hear them, though.'

Trinity walked through the palace grounds, overwhelmed with the impossibility of it all, because even a chance of future happiness for Zahid and herself would come at an appalling price.

As she wandered down towards the beach she saw the entrance to the second palace that Zahid had steered her away from.

The garden was cool and shaded but as she walked further she saw it had its own private beach.

She thought there would be guards, or workers, but there seemed to be no one and when she turned a handle on a huge carved door, as easily as that she was in.

It was agony.

A huge wooden staircase led upwards but that was not what first caught her eye. Neither were the portraits on the wall, but a glass cabinet that contained framed photos.

This was a home.

Layla was the image of Annan, who'd had smiling black eyes and the same long hair. Even Fahid looked happy but what had Trinity's eyes fill with tears was a younger Zahid.

He had even been a serious baby.

Only then, as she looked through the years, did she realise just how lucky she was to receive that smile so easily, for it would seem he shared it with few.

To torture herself she took the stairs upwards and soon found the wing that contained the master suite.

It had to be it, Trinity decided looking at the opulent bed piled with cushions, the bed where Zahid would sleep with his bride. Yes, it had to be it, Trinity thought as she opened huge shutters and stared out at the ocean, for it was a view fit for a king.

'What are you doing here?' Trinity did not jump at the sound of his voice, she was trying too hard not to turn round and to wipe her eyes without him seeing.

'Layla's taking her class. I just wanted to take a walk.' Trinity chose not to tell Zahid that they had been discussing his wedding. 'I wanted to think. I'm sorry I wandered. I never thought it would be open.'

'You don't need keys here.'

He came over and stood by her side. 'You were crying?'

Trinity nodded.

'About your brother?'

Trinity gave a soft shrug then shook her head.

'No.' She looked out at the ocean again and thought of her brother, for without him she would not be standing here. 'You know, if it weren't for his death, we would never have spoken again.'

'That is not the case,' Zahid admitted. 'I had thought about you a lot in the last month. I told you Donald asked for a loan for his honeymoon. The first time was on the night of his wedding. I refused him and offered to pay for rehab instead. The second time...' Zahid hesitated and then continued. 'It was me who called him. I did not get around to asking for your number, though. He was in a bad way and he said again that he needed a loan. If anyone should have guilt for lending money...'

Trinity turned her head. 'No.'

'I had rung every library in Los Angeles,' Zahid said, and watched as her shoulders moved in a soft laugh. 'One by one I ticked them off and in the end I rang your mother. That is how I found out that he had died.'

'Why were you trying to call me?'

'I think we both know why,' Zahid said, 'even if it must remain unsaid.'

Must it?

'Trinity, since our first kiss you have not left my mind.'

'Oh, please.' There was still anger there. 'You never gave me a thought. If Donald hadn't got married we'd never have seen each other again. You left me that night and you never looked back.' Tears were streaming down her cheeks but they were silent ones. 'You never came back.'

'I did come back,' Zahid said. 'In the new year, after your birthday. I returned, not because I wanted to spend time with your family but because I wanted to see you, but I was told that you had gone into rehab.'

'Oh, is that what they told you?' Trinity gave a mirthless laugh. 'I always wondered how they managed to explain away six months of my life.'

'Where were you?'

She couldn't discuss it, it hurt too much, but Zahid would not let it rest. 'Why would Donald and your family say you were in rehab...?' His voice trailed off as the truth started to dawn on him.

'Tell me.'

'I can't,' Trinity said.

'You can,' Zahid said. 'When will you learn that you can be honest with me?'

She had never been honest with anyone, though, for she had never been allowed to be.

'There is an Arabic proverb,' Zahid said, *'what is hidden is more than what has been revealed so far.'*

She pondered the words for a moment and they were true, so true.

The loss of her baby was, for Trinity *more* than the event that had led to her conception. She had not had to work to separate the two, for her love for her baby had brought out a fierce protectiveness in her.

'I got pregnant...' Trinity said, and then quickly added, 'Please, don't say sorry. I wanted her so much.'

Zahid said nothing, just let her continue.

'My parents wanted me to have an abortion, I just couldn't. I knew right from the start that it wasn't the baby's fault. I went away to have my baby but I lost her at six months...'

For the first time ever he felt the sting of tears

in his eyes. Even on his mother's death he had been aware he must hold things together, that he must not, even once, cry, but hearing the love in her voice, despite the pain, had the emotions Zahid despised so much coursing through him.

'Does she have a name?'

Trinity nodded. 'Amara.'

Eternal.

He did what he must not do in Ishla, he sat on the bed and pulled her into him and held her as she wept and did his best to comfort her, but Trinity was still drowning in fear, not for the baby she had lost but the one she might hold inside her now.

'You can talk to me.'

'How?' Trinity asked. 'When tonight you are dining with your future wife?'

'I will sort something out. I will buy us some time.'

'How?'

'Do you even want to be here?'

She was scared to say yes, scared to admit her truth, scared too, given how terrible it had been for her, that if she did admit her truth, if somehow she could stay, then he would forbid her from seeing her family.

'Trinity?' Zahid demanded, for he would move a mountain if he had to, but he had to know first if she wanted it moved. 'Do you want to be here?'

She stared at a man she trusted more than she had ever trusted another person, but she could not bring herself to tell him what terrified her now.

She looked into Zahid's eyes.

Her instinct was to tell him, but Trinity had been raised to deny her instincts and she did not know how to trust.

'I want to be *here*,' Trinity said, and her meaning was clear for a second later she met his mouth, her drug of choice, and it was Zahid's too and this time he could not deny her.

Their mouths were on each other's, he could taste her tears and her face was flushed from crying and her lips swollen, and it wasn't even a choice for Zahid as to whether or not he kiss her, he gave in to need.

Desperate urgent kisses that had them tear-ing at each other's clothes till they were naked and they melted into the other as their skins met again and he pressed her down onto the bed. It was dizzying, it had to be, for thought would have told them it was so very forbidden, a single thought would have warned that they could be caught at any moment, that this was wrong, very wrong. Zahid had always held onto emotion but not for a second did he hold on now.

'Tell me what you want.'

'You!' Trinity replied. It was the only answer she knew. 'This,' she said, half sitting against the cushions as he knelt between her legs. His head lowered and Zahid's mouth, hungry and rough, took her newly sensitive breasts deep, and she loved it that with Zahid pain was a new pleasure.

Then, when her breasts were not enough, when her mouth could not quench days of denial, of fighting not to react to her taunts, ended as he knelt back on his knees and pushed her legs further apart. She briefly looked down as he positioned her and then seared inside. Trinity's head went back and she was drunk on the power of him unleashed and raw as his hands moved her hips to his will.

This was Zahid's will, this was his want and even before Trinity came his decision was made and he started to spill into her.

Trinity could even feel the contractions in her womb as Zahid gave her the most intimate part of himself.

'There,' he said, and she understood his word.

'There,' he said again, as he pulsed in the final precious drops, and she forced herself forward and looked down again and watched the milky white on his length as he slowly pulled out and then drove in to her again.

It was done now.

After, they lay on the marital bed catching their breath, her hair in his mouth, her cheek hot and warm by his, and Zahid closed his eyes, but not in regret.

Tonight he dined with Princess Sameena and her family, next weekend it would be Sheikha Kumu, yet the woman he loved lay in the marital bed with him now.

It was too late to cancel the dinners, it would be considered the height of rudeness as the invitations had already been sent out.

He would get through tonight, Zahid decided but first he would speak with his father.

Foolish or not, sensible or otherwise, Zahid had chosen his bride.

His head had no say in the matter.

'I will sort this.'

Her body was so flushed she shivered as she was suddenly drenched in icy fear.

'Shouldn't I be away from here before you say anything?' Trinity was starting to panic.

'I don't want you away from me,' Zahid said. 'It's time to start trusting me, Trinity.'

'Zahid...'

'I will handle this,' Zahid said. 'I am going to make a formal request to speak with the king.'

CHAPTER TWELVE

THE KING LOOKED down from his window and saw Trinity walk out from the entrance to the second palace.

Of course she would be interested in the second palace and want to see it, the king consoled himself. After all, she had a degree in ancient art history and the second palace was rich with treasures.

There was little consolation to be had a few moments later when he watched as his rarely dishevelled son walked out.

She must leave, the king decided.

And she would be leaving tonight.

He wanted Zahid back, the man who thought only of his country, a man, the king privately admitted, who must be spared the pain that he himself had endured, for a heart was only so big.

'Is everything all right, Your Highness?'

Abdul enquired an hour or so later, when he walked in on the king, who was still deep in thought.

'It will be,' the king answered. 'What are you here for?'

'Prince Zahid has tendered a formal request to meet with you.'

Fahid's stomach churned for the words they would exchange in a formal meeting must be documented.

'I do not have time. We are to greet guests soon.'

'It is a formal request.'

'Which means I must respond by noon the next day,' the king countered, for he, better than anyone, knew the laws of his land.

'You are to arrange for Ms Foster to come and speak with me now.'

'Of course,' Abdul said obligingly. 'Though, given we are soon to receive Princess Sameena and her family, would tomorrow perhaps be a more convenient time to speak with a guest?'

No, the king thought, for this must be dealt with now and once and for all.

And the king knew how.

Zahid needed to find out just how unsuitable Trinity would be as his wife, he needed to see for himself the trouble she would cause—and tonight he would.

He turned to Abdul. 'Summon her now.'

The giddy high from making love had faded the moment Zahid had told her he would be speaking with the king.

Trinity bathed and as she came out of the bathroom her phone buzzed and Trinity let out a tense breath before answering.

'Hi, Mum,' Trinity answered. 'How are you?'

There was a long stretch of silence and it took a while for it to dawn on Trinity that her mother was crying.

'Your father wants to spread the ashes tomorrow. He wants it done but I wanted you here.'

'Who's going to be there?'

'Just family.'

'I can't, then.'

'Trinity, please…' her mother said, but without anger this time. 'I don't want to lose you.'

She might, though.

Zahid would have no part in the strange charades her family played. Zahid had already told her his thoughts on her family and that he was severing ties with them.

She loved them, though.

'You're not going to lose me but I'm not going to attend any more family functions if Clive is there.'

'Trinity—'

'I mean it.'

Finally, she did.

It was a teary Trinity that answered when Layla knocked at her door.

'I did not know that the children would upset you.'

'It was just children asking questions.' Trinity attempted a smile as she let her in.

'I know, they ask so many. All the difficult ones, of course. I did promise them that so long as they asked in English and it was a polite question, they could ask me anything.'

'Polite?' Trinity checked.

'Well, you know girls can ask difficult things and so I tell them when their question is not polite...' Layla gave an uncomfortable shrug at Trinity's questioning frown and elaborated a touch further. 'Today they ask about marriage but some of the older students ask about wedding nights and I don't think they are suitable questions.' Layla went a little bit pink. 'Or rather I don't know how to answer them.'

'I guess it could be awkward.'

'It is.' Layla admitted.

'It's good they feel they can ask questions, though.' It was Trinity's cheeks who were a bit pink now as she probed Layla for information, not that Layla could know the reason for Trinity's interest. 'I mean, where would they go here to find out about birth control and the like?' She saw Layla frown.

'Birth control?'

'If you don't want to get pregnant.'

Layla blinked. 'I thought I was the only woman who felt like that. I don't want to have Hassain's baby.'

'I meant,' Trinity swallowed as she realised the can of worms she was opening but Trinity desperately needed to guage how these issues where handled in Ishla and so she was more specific. 'What would a young woman do if she wanted to have sex but wasn't married.'

'It would never happen out of wedlock.' Layla's cheeks were on fire.

'You mean there are no unplanned babies born in Ishla?'

'Of course not,' Layla said, and Trinity just stood there as Layla continued. 'It must not happen, it cannot happen.' To Layla it was as simple as that.

But despite Layla's absolute assurance that it could never happen, it very possibly had and to the future king's potential wife.

Of course there must be unplanned pregnancies in Ishla, she knew that Layla was being naïve.

So what happened when a pregnancy occurred that wasn't planned?

Trinity did feel sick then but it was in fear for her unborn child.

Perhaps they'd insist on an abortion, just as her mother had. Only when Trinity had begged to keep her baby had she been sent away.

Zahid would do the right thing, of course, but would that be by his country or by her?

'Trinity?' Layla dragged her mind back to the conversation, her black eyes alight with curiosity. 'What is this birth control?'

Trinity was saved from answering when there was a knock at the door. It was Jamila who spoke for a moment to Layla.

'My father has requested to speak with you,' Layla told Trinity.

'It's okay,' Layla said, when Jamila had left and she saw Trinity's pale face. 'He is fierce, yes, but he is fair too, and you have done no wrong.'

But by Ishla's standards Trinity had.

CHAPTER THIRTEEN

TRINITY STEPPED INTO the study and looked to the side as she curtsied, hoping that Zahid would be here, for she did not know how to face the king alone.

'How are things?' the king asked. 'I trust you are being well looked after.'

'I've been looked after beautifully.'

'How are your family?'

'I've just spoken to my mother.'

'How is she?'

'She's a bit upset. My father wants to spread my brother's ashes.' They chatted a little about that and Trinity started to relax.

'It is a difficult time for them.'

'It is.'

'Did you enjoy your time at the second palace this afternoon?' The king saw that he had sideswiped Trinity but he would not hesitate to tackle difficult subjects when the future of his monarchy was at stake. 'Are you going to lie and say you enjoyed looking at the antiques and jewels?'

'No.'

'Is your intention to trap my son?'

Trinity had stood blushing and unable to look at the king but now her eyes did meet his. 'Trap him?'

'It is a commoners trick and you,' the king said, 'are a commoner with a past.'

'I'm not going to stand here and be insulted.'

'Where is the insult? You are a commoner, yes?'

'Yes.'

'And one with a past.'

'The insult was that I might trick your son.'

'I apologise, then,' the king answered. 'I forget that you have ways to defy nature. I would have hoped you would not bring them here but perhaps it is better that you did, for an unplanned pregnancy would bring more shame than I can even dare to imagine. More than a drug scandal.' The king gave a tight smile. 'I apologise, that was not you but your brother.'

'I would prefer, if we must discuss this, for Zahid to be here.'

'When I discuss this with my son, I will be far less polite than I am being now. I am furious with him and for the first time ever I am disappointed in him. A few weeks ago we were discussing bridges, and hospitals and the education of our people. Now he speaks only of wanting time to sort out your differences, time to see if you two might work. That is not how things work here in Ishla.' He looked at Trinity. 'We are a kind and fair country,' the king said. 'Until someone interferes in our ways.'

'You want me to leave?'

'You were always leaving, Trinity.' The king was scathing. 'Now though, it is not a question of if you leave, it is *how* you leave that matters...'

'I don't understand.'

'Then think about it,' the king said. 'I shall

arrange for a plane to take you home—is that England or America?'

'I want to speak with Zahid.'

'Of course you can speak with him, you will be joining us tonight for dinner.'

'Please, no,' Trinity begged.

'Oh, yes,' the king said. 'You can meet Princess Sameena, you can face your shame and then perhaps you will understand my rage.'

'I'll go.'

'Yes, you will, straight after dinner. And, Trinity, remember what I said. If you do care for my son, please think about what I said. It is *how* you leave that matters.

'One moment.' He paused as there was an angry knock at the door and Zahid barged in uninvited.

'Why did you summon Trinity without me?' he demanded.

'I wanted to see that she was being properly taken care of,' the king answered calmly. 'And to find out her how family was.'

'Don't!' Zahid stood livid before his father,

for he could see the paleness of Trinity's cheeks and knew she was upset. 'You do not have time to respond to a formal request for me to speak with you, yet you summon Trinity in here—'

'She was telling me that she must return to England.'

'No.' Zahid's fists were balled.

'After dinner tonight, she is leaving.'

'Oh, no.' Zahid would not put Trinity through that. He was already dreading facing Princess Sameena and he would not foist the same awkwardness on Trinity. 'If there is an issue, you discuss it with me. Trinity is not leaving tonight—'

'I am.' It was the first time she had spoken since Zahid had stormed in. The king had made it crystal clear the shame it would bring if she were to fall pregnant.

Trinity knew that she already was and she had to get away.

'I was just speaking with your father. My mother called and she's upset...' Trinity hesitated, for she knew Zahid would not let her leave if there was even a chance she might see Clive, so she chose not to tell him about the ashes. 'I think she needs me at home.'

'It isn't about what she needs.' Zahid shook his head. 'First we speak—'

'There is not time to discuss this further now.' The king stood. 'Our guests are due to arrive. I am sure Trinity will want to get ready.'

As she put on her make-up Trinity finally understood the king's wise words. Zahid loved her and he would not simply let her go, but if she stayed…

Her only thought now was for her baby. She had no idea of the rules of this land. Even Zahid had spoken of choosing a bride on the strength of an army.

The king was right. If she wanted to leave then tonight Zahid had to see for himself what an unsuitable bride she would be.

'Perhaps you wear too much…' Layla hesitated, reminding herself that Trinity was a guest but her lips worried her as Trinity put on some dark red lipstick and then added more mascara.

Trinity was wearing the lilac tunic that had been too tight even on her first day in Ishla. Her breasts seemed bigger than they had then, though Layla assumed that must be from her bra, because she caught a glimpse of it when Trinity bent forward for all the buttons were not done up.

'You missed...' Layla pointed to her own buttons as they went to head down to dinner.

Trinity ignored her.

Zahid's jaw tightened a little when he saw Trinity, not because of the glimpse of cleavage and not even because of her dark red lips. It was the dangerous glint in her eyes that had him on high alert as Trinity took her seat next to Layla.

The king made the introductions. 'This is Miss Trinity Foster, she is here to help Layla with her English. I asked her to join us so that we can say farewell to her, as she is flying back to England late tonight.'

Sameena bowed her head in greeting and

Trinity did the same, and the introductions continued.

Zahid sat silent.

Oh, there would be words at the formal meeting for putting Trinity through this.

Many, many words.

He looked at Sameena and saw her downcast eyes and Zahid's shame turned to slight curiosity, for having a sister like Layla and after the time he'd spent with Trinity, he recognised swollen eyelids when he saw them.

Perhaps Sameena did not want to be here either.

The conversation was as sticky as the dates for everyone, given that Queen Raina of Bishram was the 'suitable' bride that Fahid had rejected all those years ago.

Only Layla was oblivious to the tension.

'We were talking in my class about transport today,' Layla said, filling in a gaping hole in the conversation as dessert was served. 'Can I learn to drive, Father?'

'Why would you want to drive when you can be driven?'

'I would like to drive. Do you drive, Sameena?'

'I do.'

'Do you work?'

'Layla,' the king warned, 'it is Zahid and Sameena's time to speak with each other.'

'We must go soon,' Queen Raina said.

'Perhaps Sameena and I could walk in the gardens before you leave,' Zahid offered, and Trinity knocked over her drink.

Better that than throw it in his face, Trinity thought as a maid mopped it up.

'Layla might like to join you.' The king smiled.

'Of course,' Zahid responded, and the Queen and King of Bishram nodded their consent.

'It was a lovely dinner,' Sameena said, as Layla walked behind them.

'It was,' Zahid said. 'Were you looking forward to it?'

There was a slight hesitation before she said yes.

'Is there anything you would like to say?' Zahid carefully offered, and Sameena glanced over her shoulder at Layla.

'She is listening to her music,' Zahid said. 'She has her headphones in.'

Sameena laughed and then she stopped laughing, for it was almost an impossible conversation to have. 'My mother is talking of abdicating,' Sameena said. 'Of course, that is just between us.'

'Of course.'

'Soon I will be Queen of Bishram.'

'What is your hope for your country?'

'I have many,' Sameena said. 'Naturally, I hope that relationships between our countries will improve, whatever choice you make.' Zahid looked at her and saw tears in Sameena's eyes.

'Be honest,' Zahid said, 'because whatever you say, I look forward to better relations between our countries.'

'Even if there is anger between them for a while?' Sameena checked, for her parents would be furious with Ishla if she was not the prince's choice.

'We will work well together,' Zahid said, as they carefully forged an alliance but one that did not involve a marriage.

There was a small chink of hope in his heart as he headed back, and Trinity did not like the edge of a smile on his lips or the look that passed between Sameena and Zahid as the families said their goodbyes. It served only to confuse her.

'I need to get my things ready,' Trinity said. 'My flight is soon.'

'You are not boarding the plane tonight,' Zahid said. 'You are not leaving till I have spoken with my father.' He strode over to the king. 'I would like to speak with you now,' Zahid said to his father.

'Not yet,' Fahid said. 'I would like more coffee.'

They returned to the table and the king smiled like the cat that had got the cream. 'That went very well.'

'Really?' Zahid checked. 'I have never endured a more uncomfortable dinner.'

The king looked at Trinity. 'You have been a wonderful guest. Forgive me for not serving champagne tonight, it would have been offensive to our guests. Of course, we are more relaxed here, and it is right that we wish you farewell with a toast.'

He gestured the waiter and champagne was poured. Trinity took the smallest sip of bubbles, for she did not want them to guess the reason she could not join in with the toast properly.

Zahid didn't even raise his glass of sparkling water, for she was not leaving tonight.

Trinity caught the king's eye and as the bubbles went down she topped up her glass and it was time to ensure that she and her baby left safely tonight.

'Is Queen Raina the one you rejected in favour of your wife?'

'Trinity...' Layla breathed, for there were things that must not be openly discussed.

'I get a bit confused,' Trinity explained.

'You are correct.' The king nodded.

'You must miss your wife,' Trinity said.

'Very much.'

They chatted further and after the king said

what a wonderful, dignified woman Annan had been, the tone of the conversation moved down.

'You must get lonely,' Trinity said, and she felt the squeeze of Zahid's angry fingers on her thigh as he attempted to warn her quietly just how inappropriate that line of conversation was.

He looked at his plate and did not see the king give Trinity a small smile and he did not see the tears that flashed in Trinity's eyes. 'You're a good-looking man, Fahid. Surely...' she gave a shrill laugh '...you think about dating.'

'Perhaps I have had my time.'

'Oh, come on,' Trinity said. 'You could have your pick, a handsome man like you...'

She was flirting with his father, she was being inappropriate, and Zahid's rage simmered as again she knocked over her glass and then re-filled it.

'How would a king date?' Fahid enquired politely.

'I have no idea,' Trinity admitted. 'Where I work, at the beach bar, we have a night for the over-forties...'

'Trinity,' Zahid warned.

'What?' Trinity turned to Zahid. 'I'm just being friendly.'

'I want to speak to you alone.'

He took her wrist, pulled her away, marched her through the palace and to her room.

She could spill her drink, she could be wild, but he had never thought he'd have to tell Trinity that she could not flirt at the king's table.

He turned her to face him and his eyes were black, not with anger but with disappointment, with pain.

'What on earth was that?'

'I was just having fun.' She gave him a look. 'Oh, sorry, that's not allowed here, is it?'

'Of course it is, but tonight—'

'Oh, am I misbehaving?'

'You know that you are.'

'So I'm just supposed to sit quietly while you go for a walk with your future bride, while you make simpering eyes when you say goodbye to her—'

'Do not even suggest that I flirted with Princess Sameena,' Zahid said. 'Tonight I have done everything I know how to secure us some time together, I have spoken with Sameena, I have asked for a formal meeting with my father and then you sit there, pissed, and you flirt with my father, the king.'

'I had two glasses,' Trinity lied, for she'd had none.

'Is that all it takes for you to act like a tart?' Zahid demanded. 'I don't get you, Trinity.'

'I never asked you to,' Trinity said. 'Am I not being respectful enough for you?'

'No,' Zahid said. 'You are not being respectful to yourself.'

'Don't worry, in an hour or so I won't be your problem any more.'

'Go to bed,' Zahid said.

'What?'

'You heard. Go to bed and I will speak with you tomorrow.'

Even at her supposed worst, he would not let her leave, Trinity realised.

Zahid, her eyes begged, let me go, for she was

terrified what would happen if the king found out she was with child, not just for herself but for the shame it would heap on Zahid.

'Bed,' Zahid said.

'My flight—'

'Will be cancelled.'

'I want to go home.'

'You are not leaving now. It will all be sorted tomorrow,' Zahid continued, 'once and for all.'

'What if I don't want it to be sorted?' The grip on her arm loosened. 'What if I don't want to be your chosen bride.'

'I understand that you—'

'You *don't* understand,' Trinity choked, because for the first time in her life it was almost impossible to lie. 'Because you've never asked.'

'I thought we felt the same.'

'No,' Trinity said. 'We don't. I don't want to be your bride.'

'You're sure?'

'Very sure.'

Zahid gave a curt nod and she watched as the beautiful man she knew literally disappeared before her eyes, for he was back to yawn-yawn dignified in that second.

'I will have a maid come and sort out your things.'

CHAPTER FOURTEEN

IN A LAND where emotions were considered best contained, it was Layla who broke the rules, for she sobbed loudly as the driver arrived to take Trinity the short distance to the royal jet. 'I will come with you to the plane.'

'We'll say goodbye here,' Trinity said, and hugged her hard. She would miss Layla so much.

She gave a small curtsy to the king, who gave her a brief nod in return, and then she stood before Zahid and did not know how to say goodbye.

'I will see you to the plane.'

This time she did not refuse.

It was a very short drive to the runway, but if it had been a hundred miles it would have gone by too fast for she was saying goodbye not just to Zahid but her baby's father too.

'I am sorry for my behaviour tonight.'

'It was funny really.' Zahid gave a pale smile. 'I'm sure my father has not enjoyed himself so much in years.'

'You're not cross?'

'Temporarily,' Zahid said, 'then you make me laugh.' He was not laughing now and he only ever had with her. 'I apologise for assuming,' Zahid said, as the car pulled up at the plane. 'I assumed this madness was mutual.'

'Madness?'

'That's what it feels like,' Zahid said, and then he looked at her. 'I enjoyed being briefly insane.'

'You can go back to normal now.'

'I can.'

She went to embrace him but Zahid pulled back. He was gone from her now. 'You will have a safe flight.'

'Will?'

'You are on my plane. Do you need anything?'

'No.'

'You have not worked, you gave all your money to Donald.'

'I'll be fine.'

Sometimes the apple did fall far from the tree.

'I don't know what to say,' Zahid said. 'I never expected to be saying goodbye.'

Would she call him? Trinity wondered as she looked into his eyes. Would she tell him from the safety of England?

Would it be cruel to do so?

For now she just needed to leave.

'Look after yourself better,' Zahid said. 'You have every right to stay away from that man.'

Trinity blew out a breath.

If her mother had her way, she'd be seeing Clive tomorrow.

No.

'I'm going to go,' Trinity said.

If she didn't she might just tell Zahid how much she loved him.

The king watched as his son returned to the palace and he felt a rare prick of guilt when he saw the confusion in Zahid's eyes, for he had not seen that look since Zahid had been seven and the king had lain in a stupor.

'Happy now?' Zahid shot at his father, as he headed up the stairs.

'You will be,' Fahid said. 'It hurts to lose someone you care for.'

'Don't you ever try to give me advice on this.'

'Her behaviour tonight was shocking.'

'Not to me.' Zahid halted on his climb up the stairs and turned. 'She pushes boundaries, she tests you at every turn, she wants to prove she is right in that she cannot trust you. If you knew what she had been through...' Zahid shook his head. He had never wanted less to be a future king. 'I'm going to bed.'

'We will speak in the morning.'

'We will speak when I am ready to,' Zahid said, 'and that might take some time.'

'There are dinners...'

'Cancel them.'

'Zahid.' The king attempted reason. 'Trinity needs to be with her family. It is right she be with them now. Tomorrow they spread the ashes...'

The king was not scared of danger, he had an army of his own and he would happily lead them, but as Zahid descended the stairs he caught a glimpse of fear.

'What did you say?'

'Her mother called. She wants her to join her family to spread the ashes.'

No.

A thousand times no.

Whether she wanted his love or not, he wouldn't let that happen.

'Why wouldn't she tell me that?' Zahid asked himself out loud.

A lie by omission, but still a lie.

He could not believe a single word that came from her mouth, Zahid realised, which meant that saying she did not want to be his bride might also be a lie.

Oh, there was unfinished business between them again and he was not going to wait months or years to address it this time—another sun would not set without this being sorted.

'I am going to England.'

The King stared at him. 'I forbid you.'

'Then I defy you,' Zahid said.

'You cannot defy me.' The king stared at his son but could only admire him.

'You raised me to be strong.'

'You turn your back on our people, our traditions…'

'If I have to, yes.' Zahid nodded. 'Right now, there is someone that I need to be with and I refuse to have her face things alone.'

'You select a bride in a few days…'

'Perhaps I already have.'

'She is not suitable.'

'For who?' Zahid said. 'She is more than suitable for me.'

'You know the rules.'

'Change them,' Zahid challenged. 'Is that not the point of being a king?'

'It is not as simple as that…'

'It's very simple for me,' Zahid said.

'Our people would not welcome her.'

'They would if you did.'

'And if she won't live here?'

'That is something Trinity and I will discuss but without an ancient rule book over our heads. I am going to England now.'

'She has your plane.'

'Then I will take a commercial flight.'

'Your judgment is blinded by lust.'

'No,' Zahid said. 'My judgement is *clarified* by love.'

'A king must first love his country.'

'Don't worry, Father. I will not repeat your mistakes.' Zahid stared his father down, and brought up what must never be discussed. 'Love did not weaken you, Father, it was her death that you could not cope with.' Fahid had not struck his son in decades but his hand was raised now. 'You could not cope,' Zahid said, 'but I did.' He looked at his father who stood with his arm raised. 'I was seven and I coped with the death of my mother. I dealt with your daughter who you could not bear to look at, I fed you with a spoon when you had no will to live.' Zahid understood then his father's fear for his children but it made little sense. 'Would you rather not have chosen her?'

'Of course not.'

'Do you regret a single day spent with your wife?'

'Only her last day,' Fahid admitted. 'I did not understand her pain, I thought it was normal for women to scream when giving birth...'

'So did the doctor,' Zahid challenged his father's guilt. 'And the doula too. You lost the woman you loved through no fault of your own. Well, I refuse to play a part in losing the woman that I love.'

Zahid turned from his father and went to walk out and to summon his driver, but the king called him back. 'You could have the plane turned around.'

'If Trinity returns to Ishla, it will be of her own accord.'

Fahid gave in then and looked at his son with slightly shocked eyes, for the day had come where his son was stronger and more knowing than he, a day that for any parent was a challenge, especially when you were king.

'Zahid.' The king halted him again. 'There is something that perhaps you should know. Tonight, when Trinity was being inappropriate—'

'I will discuss the behaviour with Trinity, I do not have to discuss it with you. She does not know how to behave on occasion but—'

'Trinity knew exactly what she was doing,' the king interrupted, 'because I asked her to misbehave.'

Zahid frowned.

'I encouraged her poor behaviour. I thought it would be easier on you in the end if you saw just how unsuitable she was.'

'When you say you encouraged, did you and Trinity discuss this?'

'We did.'

'Could I remind you that though you are my father and king—'

'And sick,' the king added hastily, for he could

see the muscle leaping in Zahid's cheek and that his fist was clenched.

'Lucky for you!' Zahid retorted, but it strangled near the end and the king did not now fear his son, instead he was devastated for him. For the first time there were tears in Zahid's eyes and that was something Fahid had thought he would never see.

'Take my plane,' the king said, and for the first time since before Annan had died he embraced his son. 'Go to her now.'

CHAPTER FIFTEEN

ZAHID HAD BEEN angry about many things involving Trinity, but he had never been truly angry with her.

That changed as his plane streaked through the sky, trying to make up the hours between them.

Over and over he replayed last night.

The snap of jealousy about his walk with Sameena did not equate with a woman who did not want him.

Little liar, Zahid said to himself.

He should have known when his father had produced champagne that something was going on. And, no, she had not had even two glasses, for he had never met anyone more clumsy than Trinity last night and she had knocked over her glass...

Every detail he replayed and, apart from once, that glass had not touched her lips.

He thought of her cleavage and it had either been one helluva push-up bra or Trinity was pregnant.

Was that why she had run?

Was he so formidable that she could not share the truth?

He was formidable now!

Trinity arrived at Heathrow still dressed in the lilac dress and wearing jewelled slippers, and she startled when she caught her reflection in the mirror as she stepped into the VIP lounge, because what had started to feel normal felt very different here.

Assuming she would be heading for a taxi rank, Trinity soon found out that luxury didn't end at the landing of a royal flight.

A driver was waiting and he asked her where she wanted to go. She asked that he take her the short distance to the airport hotel.

As she went to check in, instead of asking for

a shoebox, Trinity splurged and asked for a nice suite as she pulled out her credit card.

Well, not splurged.

She was simply tired of scrimping and foreseeing disaster and crisis when, really, the disasters and crises had not been of her own making.

When she should possibly be feeling at her most vulnerable and weakest, Trinity felt the strongest she ever had.

Things changed today.

Trinity stepped into the shower and decided that if her family wanted her there at such things, there were conditions that needed to be met.

And if they weren't met then her family would not be seeing the child she was carrying.

It was suddenly as simple as that.

Her time with Zahid had made her stronger rather than weaker; his absolute honesty made it easier for Trinity to know her truth.

She was too numb to start mourning their relationship, too focused on getting through today to break down.

She put on the hotel robe and tied a towel round her head and was just sorting out the black clothes to wear for the spreading of the ashes later in the day when there was a knock at the door.

Assuming it was breakfast or someone to come and check the mini-bar before she let loose on the chocolate, Trinity opened the door without thinking and came face to face with a Zahid she had never seen.

Oh, she'd seen him angry on occasion but not once, despite all her shenanigans, despite all she had done, never, Trinity realised, had his anger been aimed at her.

It was now.

'How did you know where I was?'

She stood back as he marched in and tossed down his case and there was the same start of surprise at the sight of him in robes that Trinity had felt when she'd seen her own reflection in the mirror at Heathrow.

In England she'd only ever seen him in a suit and being terribly polite.

'Did you collude with my father?' He towered over her and she tried to stand her ground.

'I think "collude" is a bit of a strong word...' Trinity attempted.

'Did the two of you decide that you thought you knew what was best for me?'

'No,' Trinity said. 'We thought, or rather I knew, you were struggling...'

'Struggling?' Zahid frowned. 'What do you mean, struggling?'

'With the decision—' his temper wasn't improving, she could hear his angry breathing '—as to my suitability, so I thought—'

'You thought you'd make it easier for me?'

'Yes.'

'You thought you'd flirt with my father and pretend to be drunk and that that would improve matters?' Zahid said, and Trinity swallowed. 'You thought you that if you misbehaved I'd decide you were too much trouble?'

'I guess.'

'Why don't we stop guessing?'

'Zahid, the sex is amazing and all that but it's not going to carry us—'

'You think you're so good in bed that you defy my logic?'

'No,' Trinity said. 'Maybe.'

'You think my judgement is skewed?'

'A bit!'

'What, because I don't just say to hell with it, just because I don't decide on a whim to discard everything I have ever believed in, without due thought, you assume I am struggling.'

No, but she could not tell him that without revealing her truth.

She just didn't know how to tell him.

'Is there anything else you haven't told me?'

'No.'

'Are you sure about that?'

'Completely.'

Zahid picked up her black clothes. 'Where are you off to today?'

'I haven't made up my mind.'

'Do you want to be my bride?'

'No.'

'I'll take that as a yes,' Zahid said, 'because not one honest word has come from your lips since last night. Do you love me?'

'Is it a yes-or-no answer only?'

'Trinity!'

'Yes.' Trinity smiled. 'Yes, Zahid, I love you, but given I'm clearly a compulsive liar...'

She did the wrong thing. Trinity started to laugh at her own joke. 'Zahid,' she yelped, 'what are you—?'

She never got to finish.

Trinity had been tipped over his shoulder once before but it was different this time, she was being tipped over his knee.

'What I should have done a long time ago,' Zahid said. 'Three times I have come back for you and still you doubt me. I tell you this much! I put up with your drama and your carry-on.' His hand came down on her bottom through the thick dressing gown and Trinity shrieked, her hands moving to cover her bottom, but he brushed them away and gave her another slap.

'You do not make decisions about us without

speaking with me.' His hand came down again and the wad of material was a hindrance so he ruched it up and brought his hand down on her bare pink cheeks. It stung, it hurt, but the passion that came with the delivery felt delicious to Trinity as he slapped her again.

'You do not lie to me,' he said, as his hand went to come down again and then stilled. Zahid halted, barely able to breathe as he looked down at her red bottom and realised for the first time he was out of control. 'Trinity...' His hand was in mid-air and he waited for her to shout, to tell him what a sick bastard he was, and then he heard her voice.

'One more, Captain.'

He rarely laughed and he'd never thought he'd be laughing this morning. He was angry, though, still angry as he tipped her off his knee and onto the bed.

'I nearly came,' Trinity said. She was lying there, smiling up at him, watching as he stripped, and nothing was going to tame her and nothing could in this moment tame him.

'You are impossible,' he said to a very over-excited Trinity.

'You chose impossible,' Trinity said. 'Can we talk about this later?'

It wouldn't be much later for he was over her, and he did not need to part her legs for they wrapped around his hips in glee as his mouth crushed hers.

'The last one was true,' Trinity said, as he bucked inside her.

'I know.'

'How?' she begged as he as he thrust deeper. 'How do you know I love you?'

'Because…' His words halted as the sob from Trinity and the throb of her around him told him she might not hear his words, but he said them anyway. 'Because of this.' His answer released into her and it really was a simple as that, for with no one, ever, could it be so lovely. Only Zahid could right a million wrongs.

'Never leave me,' Trinity said, as he collapsed onto her.

'I never will.'

'I'll get things wrong.'

'Oh, I am sure you will.'

'Your father…'

'I have dealt with him,' Zahid said. 'You did not have to run away. Whatever our problems, we can work them out.'

Her eyes filled with tears because the reason that she had run was coming back to Trinity now; the reason for her terror was a secret she could no longer keep.

'Is there anything you are keeping from me?' Zahid said, only very gently this time.

'Yes.'

Finally, Zahid thought, the truth.

'I know you said it must never happen, I know I promised it wouldn't…' She could barely get the words out. 'I'm pregnant.'

She waited for anger, a slap even, just as her mother had, but instead Zahid pulled her tighter in his arms.

'That is why you left?'

Trinity nodded.

'You felt you could not tell me?' Zahid looked at her and how he rued that stupid slit-throat gesture he had made that day, given all that she had been through, and he answered for her. 'Of course you thought you couldn't.'

'You're not cross.'

'I'm thrilled.'

Trinity wasn't particularly used to anyone she loved being thrilled by her *mistakes*.

'I am sad that you could not come and tell me but I understand why.'

'Your father asked if I was trying to trap you,' Trinity explained. 'He saw us leaving the second palace.'

'You got one of his pep talks!' Zahid rolled his eyes. 'Do I look trapped?'

Trinity shook her head. 'I asked Layla about unplanned pregnancies and she said it could never happen…'

'Layla has never been out of Ishla. Layla believes everything that is told to her simply because she does not know any different. My father wraps her in cotton wool and terrifies her with tales in the hope she will be too scared to ever make a mistake.' Zahid looked at her.

'How many times do I have to tell you that you can come to me?'

'I know,' Trinity said. 'I was just too scared to in this.'

'Never be scared to come to me.'

She looked at Zahid and knew she would never be scared again.

'I want you as my wife,' Zahid said. 'The decision is actually a very easy one, yet I have forced myself to question it many times. I never wanted love, I thought it had destroyed my father, but I was wrong.' He tried to explain better. 'I love my country, I wanted a clear head to rule it, yet my head has never been clearer than it is now. You distract me in a way that is good. It makes me want change, to tackle issues that are difficult, to rule not just with my head but with my heart.'

'What will the people say about the baby?'

'Most will be thrilled, some will say we bring disgrace, others will know we are not so different from their own families...' He smiled at Trinity. 'Controversy is good,' Zahid said. 'It allows for discussion and I think you are going to be a very controversial queen but a very good one.'

'What will your father say?'

'I have been spending too much time with you because suddenly I have the strange compulsion to lie.' He looked at her. 'Shall we tell him after the wedding? Would that make things easier for you?'

'It would.'

'What else are you scared of? What else do you think you can't discuss with me?'

'Nothing.'

'You're sure?'

Honesty had never been on Trinity's agenda. The way she had been brought up had been about smoothing over the bumps with lies, ignoring problems in the hope they would disappear, not sharing the scary, shameful parts.

It was time to change.

'I love my family.' She didn't know how best to describe it. 'They've lost their son, I don't want them to feel that they've lost their daughter too. I can't turn my back on them and I will go to family events.'

'Of course,' Zahid said, 'so what is worrying you?'

'You,' Trinity admitted. 'That you'll cause a scene, say something…'

'It is beyond unfair of your parents to expect you to see this man.'

Trinity looked at him and, yes, at times she was grateful for his excellent self-control and knew he was exerting it now.

'I'd already decided that,' Trinity admitted. 'I was going to ring them and tell them that if they wanted me there today then he wasn't to be.'

'Was?'

'I think we should just get through today and then I'll…' she screwed her eyes closed. 'I don't know what I want.'

'Maybe you need to tell him face to face that you don't want him around,' Zahid said, for clearly she could not rely on her parents to defend her as parents should.

He looked at her as she spoke.

'I don't ever want to speak to him.'

'Are you sure?' Zahid said, 'because I will deal with it if that is what you want.'

'That's not what I want.' She looked back at a very pensive Zahid and, no, she could not put him through this for the rest of their lives, could not ask him to attend functions and stand idly by.

'You don't have to be drunk to take to the microphone,' Zahid said.

'I wasn't drunk that night.'

He smiled in dispute.

'A bit maybe,' Trinity admitted.

'Well, you don't have to be to say what is on your mind.'

'If I do say something…'

'I'll be there.'

'I'd prefer you wait here at the hotel.'

Zahid shook his head.

'In the car, then.'

'No,' Zahid said. 'You are not facing this without me.'

'So, on top of everything else, I have to worry about you losing your head...'

'I won't lose my head,' Zahid said. 'You have my word.'

If ever she was grateful for Zahid's self-control it was today. It made Trinity strong when she questioned her own, it kept her calm enough to face what she had been unable to before.

Zahid dressed in an immaculate suit and Trinity had on her funeral clothes, but they were facing a difficult day together this time.

Zahid waved away his driver, for he could see she felt awkward enough, and he drove them himself. As he did, Trinity mind flitted to anything other than what lay ahead.

'Poor Sameena...' She turned in sudden anguish. 'What will happen to the two countries?'

'A war perhaps,' Zahid said, then he stopped teasing her. 'Had you not decided to escape you would have found out that Sameena and I had a very polite conversation.'

'In the garden?'

Zahid nodded. 'Soon Sameena will be Queen

and she looks forward to happy relations between our countries, whatever my choice. It was a very discreet conversation but reading between the lines she was asking me not to choose her.'

'She rejected you!' Trinity beamed.

'You're going to get so much mileage out of that,' Zahid sighed.

'I am,' Trinity said, and then stopped smiling, for Zahid was pulling up at the river that had been chosen for the occasion. It was a place the family had gone for drives to at times and where Donald had proposed to Yvette.

'Ready?' Zahid checked, and Trinity nodded.

'You can do this.'

'I don't think Yvette knows…'

'Well, let her find out,' Zahid said. 'Maybe some honesty will allow her to speak more openly about what she has been through. Her baby and ours are going to be cousins. Don't you want them to be close?'

'I do.'

'Lies haven't worked for a long time,' Zahid said. 'Maybe you could try the truth.'

'You promise that you won't—'

'I will not lose my head.'

He took her hand and they walked over to the small gathering, but as he went to give her hand a squeeze to offer support her fingers slipped away from his grasp, just not in the way they had on that awful night all those years ago. Instead of reaching out in fear to Zahid, it was an assertive Trinity who walked towards the small crowd.

'What's he doing here?' Trinity asked, pointing her finger at Clive. 'Why on earth would you ask the man who attacked your seventeen-year-old daughter to be here on this day?'

'Trinity!' Dianne said. 'Not now.'

'When, then?'

'Trinity,' Dianne said in low tones as Gus tried to hush her, but finally Trinity refused to be hushed.

'Why are we whispering?' Trinity said. 'I mean it, I want to remember my brother today.

I want to think about Donald instead of remembering what this sleaze did to me that night.' She looked at Clive and she saw not a strong, angry man but the pathetic, weak creep that he was. 'I don't ever want to see you again and if I do, I'll be going to the police. And I don't give a damn what it will do to my family, or to your reputation, because I know what you did to me and I'm more than prepared to say it in court.'

'Come on, Clive.' Elaine started to walk off. 'She was always trouble,' she shouted over her shoulder, 'always making stuff up.'

'For God's sake, Trinity,' Gus boomed, 'it's your brother's...'

'I just want to say one thing.' Zahid's deep voice was out of place with the shouting but even Trinity shivered at the sinister calm of his voice. 'I promised Trinity that I would not lose my head today and I shall keep my word.' He might be in Western clothes but he was a dangerous desert warrior and had she been on the end of his look that was aimed at Clive, Trinity would have run for her life. 'If my gaze ever falls on you again then know I shall keep my word to Trinity and not lose my head, because I won't need to. I will kill you in cold blood.'

'He doesn't mean it...' Dianne's smile was frantic but Zahid's cool disdain met her now.

'You can test the theory if you choose but, I tell you once, my people would expect nothing less from their future king.'

He watched every step that Clive took as he walked off and it was at the right moment that Trinity took his hand because the master of self-control was waning as Clive took one final look around. Trinity felt the zip of tension in Zahid, knew that at any second he'd change his mind and bolt after him, and perhaps Clive sensed it too for he ran the last of the distance to the car and Zahid turned and looked at Dianne.

'I do mean it.' He put his arm around Trinity and they walked down to the river.

It was nice to be able to focus on her brother today, nice to recall the good times with Zahid by her side, and it was actually, for the first time, nice to step into her home.

'Why has Zahid asked to speak alone with your father?' Dianne asked.

'You'll find out soon.'

'Should I check if there's champagne in the fridge?'

'Zahid doesn't drink,' Trinity said, and then smiled at her mum. 'And there's always champagne in the fridge.'

'I'm sorry, Trinity.'

From out of the blue they came—the words she'd never thought she'd hear.

'Thank you.'

'Can we start again?' Dianne asked.

'I think we have to.'

They did start again, right from square one, because after a quiet celebration where they shared the news that they would be married soon, it was not long before Trinity yawned and said she wanted to go to bed.

'Perhaps set up…' Dianne's voice broke off.

'Zahid will sleep with me,' Trinity said, 'or we can go back to the hotel.'

Zahid did not correct Trinity, for to hell

with politeness, he would never set foot in the guest room.

He wished them goodnight and they headed to her single bed.

'What did she say?' Zahid smiled as they huddled in the darkness. 'When you started laughing in the kitchen?'

'It was wrong,' Trinity blushed. 'I can't tell you.'

'You can.'

'Okay.' Trinity took a big breath. 'Mum said that when your father dies, will she have a title?'

'She wants a title?'

'She's wants to be the Queen Mother.'

He laughed.

It was rare, it was deep and it thrilled her right down to her bones, and there would be so much more of it, Trinity would make sure of that.

'How could I have ever thought you boring?' Trinity sighed.

'Another thing you haven't told me,' Zahid said. 'When did you think I was boring?'

'For years,' Trinity said. 'Till you took me in your arms.'

EPILOGUE

'WHERE'S TRINITY?'

Zahid heard the whisper from Dianne as he stood in the palace gardens, waiting for his bride to arrive, and, yes, she was more than fashionably late.

Zahid stared ahead. He was dressed in military ceremonials with a red and white *kafiya* tied with gold braid, which indicated he was the groom. His concern was not that Trinity might have changed her mind, his concern was for all she faced not just today but in the two days preceding the wedding.

He stood with his back rigid, feeling all the eyes of the guests on him. It was forbidden that they see each other in the lead-up to the wedding. Tradition did not take into account that the news of the future princess's pregnancy might have broken forty-eight hours before the wedding service.

Tonight they would be in the desert, Zahid thought.

Tonight, whatever the people's reaction to Trinity, he could put her mind at ease and then, in a week's time, they were heading overseas.

As the guests coughed anxiously Zahid actually managed a smile. He had asked Trinity where she would like to go for her honeymoon and, even though they were getting on much better, her answer had been as far away from her parents as possible, so they were heading for Australia. He simply couldn't wait to get away with his bride. The only teeny fly in the ointment was that he had promised that Layla could join them for a week.

Love had been the furthest thing from his mind when he had agreed to that.

It was the closest thing now.

He had watched his father's skin pale when the scandalous news had first hit and, no, when the king had called for him, Zahid had not denied it.

As strong as he was, guilt had washed over him as he'd seen his father, so old and so thin, struggle to take in the latest change.

'I am sorry if you feel I have let down you and my mother's memory.'

'Your mother was as vague as your sister now is,' the king sighed. 'I went through the mandoos last night and I thought how she would be with the news. I held her favourite amulet and I just knew that she would have been delighted.'

Fahid called in Abdul, who immediately said he would issue the strongest denial.

'You shall neither confirm or deny,' the king said, and Zahid watched as Abdul's face paled when he realised the rumour was true, and then the king said the strangest thing to Zahid.

Words he could not wait to share with Trinity.

Yet he had not been able to get to her yet.

'I am so excited.' Layla's endless chatter did nothing to ease Trinity's nerves. 'You don't mind me coming to Australia with you?'

'Of course not.'

'I'm only there for a week…'

'It will be wonderful,' Trinity said, but she could not focus on Layla's conversation or the maids who were doing her hair. Outside the crowd was building and they stood silent, awaiting the news of the formal union.

Layla's chatter was not selfish. She was trying to take Trinity's mind off her pregnancy being referred to as a scandal in some of the papers and that Ishla was alight not just with wedding preparations but with the news that Zahid's bride might already be with child.

At the time she needed to speak with Zahid most, to finally lean on someone she trusted, it was denied. 'Have you seen your father today?'

'No,' Layla said. 'The men's and women's celebrations are kept separate.'

'You must have heard something.'

Layla went a little bit pink. She still felt guilty and a little embarrassed by her naïve reaction when Trinity had clearly needed her advice.

Obviously this birth control thing Trinity had spoke of did not work!

'Only what I told you. Zahid asked one of the maids to pass on that you were not to be concerned, to just enjoy the celebrations and that you would be together soon.'

Trinity knew that Zahid would be there for her and no doubt he would already have discussed the revelation with the king. Zahid's rapid departure from Ishla had been noted and there had been an image of them coming out a famous obstetrician's office. As well as that, despite a hastily arranged wedding, despite the gold gown she was wearing, given that it was her second pregnancy, Trinity was already starting to show.

Only it wasn't the king's reaction that worried her, or the damage to Zahid. It was the how the people would respond that gnawed at Trinity. Their reaction mattered, not because it changed the outcome but because it might change how Trinity felt towards them. She had already had one pregnancy steeped in shame, she refused to let this be another.

'You look beautiful,' Layla said, as Trinity stood to have her headwear arranged.

'Thank you.'

'We need to go,' Layla said. 'You are already late.'

'I'll just be a moment.'

Trinity had been raised to care only what others thought, and what others thought mattered terribly now.

No, it didn't.

Trinity knew that their baby had been conceived in love, knew that Zahid and she were meant to be together. Since that night in the woods their love had waited patiently till the time had been right, and she had to trust the timing of their baby had been chosen too.

Trinity peeked out at the silent crowd, who gave no indication as to their response to her.

She would find that out on the balcony.

Right now she had a wedding to attend and she wanted to be there.

Zahid turned as she arrived and it was not the Trinity he had been expecting. Instead of being wary and truculent, her eyes shone with confidence and as her eyes met his her cheeks infused with pink as they did whenever she saw him.

And, yes, the papers would confirm that the rumours were surely right, for the soft breeze pushed the fabric of her dress and there was the curve of her stomach.

Zahid smiled, and, just as she had been at Donald's wedding, so lost was she that she did as her body instructed and walked to be by his side.

'You look amazing.'

'Thank you.'

He had expected a hurried question, to ask if all was well.

It was.

Whatever the ramifications, they would face them together.

The service was quick, given that it was held in the fierce midday sun, but the part she would always remember best was after Zahid made his vows and then offered her a bracelet that had an Arabic saying engraved in English.

'I mean it,' he said as she read what was inscribed inside.

What is coming is better than what is gone.

With Zahid it was always better, Trinity knew.

There was no kissing his bride. Instead, he took her hand and led her back to the palace.

Trinity smiled at her parents and at Yvette, who was a few months ahead of Trinity in her pregnancy.

They were friends now and, as Zahid had pointed out, their children would be cousins.

She would be taken care of too.

There was Princess Sameena, who curtsied to the new princess as her parents stood severely at her side, and they shared a small smile, for the future of both their countries was so bright.

The rest of the guests followed them and still Trinity did not ask his father's reaction to the news.

'We meet the people now,' Zahid said, and

squeezed her hand. The memory of Trinity scowling at the camera did not make him smile now. He was, not that he could show it, worried by the reception from the people. He did not want their wedding day to be one where he asked her to force a smile. 'It won't take long.' Zahid cleared his throat. 'If they are a little hesitant, know that soon they will take to the news...' He frowned as she simply nodded and Zahid actually wondered if she had been shielded from the scandal that had hit Ishla. 'They may—'

'Zahid,' Trinity said, 'I'm not going to apologise or be ashamed.'

'Good.'

As the balcony doors opened and they went to step out, they were halted, as instead of the happy couple leading the way King Fahid did instead.

Zahid blinked.

His father had at that meeting reminded his son that he was still king and that he would sort it.

Zahid had wondered how.

Now he knew, for Fahid walked out onto the balcony to the surprise of the people and met them with a smile they had not seen on his face since before Princess Layla had been born.

He held out an arm and welcomed the couple.

'He welcomed the news,' Zahid said, and Trinity swallowed.

'Really?'

'It took only an hour for him to say that he could not be happier. He does not have much time and this way he gets to meet our child...'

With the king's clear blessing, as the happy couple stepped onto the balcony they were met with cheers and waves. The silence had been broken for things that had never been discussed in Ishla were being talked about now.

How, Trinity wondered, as Zahid now kissed his bride, could she rue the years that had been wasted?

Time knew best.

They were together now.

* * * * *

Mills & Boon® Large Print
January 2015

THE HOUSEKEEPER'S AWAKENING
Sharon Kendrick

MORE PRECIOUS THAN A CROWN
Carol Marinelli

CAPTURED BY THE SHEIKH
Kate Hewitt

A NIGHT IN THE PRINCE'S BED
Chantelle Shaw

DAMASO CLAIMS HIS HEIR
Annie West

CHANGING CONSTANTINOU'S GAME
Jennifer Hayward

THE ULTIMATE REVENGE
Victoria Parker

INTERVIEW WITH A TYCOON
Cara Colter

HER BOSS BY ARRANGEMENT
Teresa Carpenter

IN HER RIVAL'S ARMS
Alison Roberts

FROZEN HEART, MELTING KISS
Ellie Darkins

MILLS & BOON®
Large Print – February 2015

AN HEIRESS FOR HIS EMPIRE
Lucy Monroe

HIS FOR A PRICE
Caitlin Crews

COMMANDED BY THE SHEIKH
Kate Hewitt

THE VALQUEZ BRIDE
Melanie Milburne

THE UNCOMPROMISING ITALIAN
Cathy Williams

PRINCE HAFIZ'S ONLY VICE
Susanna Carr

A DEAL BEFORE THE ALTAR
Rachael Thomas

THE BILLIONAIRE IN DISGUISE
Soraya Lane

THE UNEXPECTED HONEYMOON
Barbara Wallace

A PRINCESS BY CHRISTMAS
Jennifer Faye

HIS RELUCTANT CINDERELLA
Jessica Gilmore

0115 Rom LP

MILLS & BOON®

Why shop at millsandboon.co.uk?

Each year, thousands of romance readers find their perfect read at millsandboon.co.uk. That's because we're passionate about bringing you the very best romantic fiction. Here are some of the advantages of shopping at www.millsandboon.co.uk:

* **Get new books first**—you'll be able to buy your favourite books one month before they hit the shops

* **Get exclusive discounts**—you'll also be able to buy our specially created monthly collections, with up to 50% off the RRP

* **Find your favourite authors**—latest news, interviews and new releases for all your favourite authors and series on our website, plus ideas for what to try next

* **Join in**—once you've bought your favourite books, don't forget to register with us to rate, review and join in the discussions

Visit **www.millsandboon.co.uk**
for all this and more today!